Heartland

༃

Everything Changes

Heartland

❧

Share every moment. . . .

Heartland

Everything Changes

by Lauren Brooke

SCHOLASTIC INC.

New York   Toronto   London   Auckland   Sydney
Mexico City   New Delhi   Hong Kong   Buenos Aires

ISBN 0-439-42509-3

Heartland series created by Working Partners Ltd, London.

Copyright © 2003 by Working Partners Ltd.
Published by Scholastic Inc. All rights reserved.

SCHOLASTIC and associated logos are trademarks and/or registered trademarks of Scholastic Inc. HEARTLAND is a trademark and/or registered trademark of Working Partners Ltd.

12 11 10 9 8 7 6 5 4 3 2 1   3 4 5 6 7 8/0
Printed in the U.S.A.   40
First printing, December 2003

With special thanks to Gill Harvey

Dedicated to my dear friends Dawn, Kate, Abbey, and Jamie, who "changed their everythings" when they moved from Scotland to New Zealand in October 2002. I love them very much.

Heartland

❧

Everything Changes

Chapter One

The little bay pony's hooves thundered over the grass as she stretched her legs into a full gallop. Laughing out loud, Amy leaned forward, the wind rippling through her hair. As they approached the crest of Clairdale Ridge, Amy sat up in the saddle and eased the pony back to a trot.

"Steady, Willow," she said. "Easy does it."

Willow arched her neck and snorted, responding willingly to Amy. At the top of the ridge, they halted and looked out over the view. It was stunning. The morning mist hadn't fully cleared, and thin wisps still drifted through the valley below, floating gently over the autumn colors of red, gold, and copper that tinged the trees.

Amy stroked Willow's neck, smiling to herself. Willow

1

was so different now — relaxed, confident, and happy to have a rider on her back. Amy remembered when, not so long ago, Willow had been a terrified, shattered creature, too afraid to let anyone near her. Helping her to recover had taken Amy weeks of patient care and encouragement — but that was what Heartland was all about.

Amy turned Willow, and they started walking down the path, back toward Heartland, its stables, and paddocks. Willow's stride became light and springy as they neared the farm, and Amy felt sorry for the pony. After all these weeks, Willow thought that the Heartland horse sanctuary was home — but that wasn't the way things worked. Considering the pony's progress, Amy knew that Willow would soon be going back to her owners, making room for another pony or horse in need.

They rode past the paddocks and the back barn, both of which had been rebuilt following a recent storm. Amy closed her eyes as the memory of that terrible night swept over her. She could still hear the howling wind, the creak of the wooden beams in the barn, and the scared, shrill whinnies of the horses trapped inside. Her grandfather's words echoed in her mind, the words he had spoken to Ty and Amy as they went in to rescue the panicking horses. *If there's any movement at all in the roof, you must get out immediately*. But they hadn't — Amy and

Ty had been too focused on the horses — and the beams had given way, crashing down and engulfing everything in sight. Amy shivered slightly, feeling her heart twist in pain. One of the horses, Dylan, had been killed, and Ty had been in a coma ever since the barn collapsed.

Amy missed Ty terribly. He was the lead stable hand at Heartland and the only other person who understood the special, alternative methods they used for treating horses. But he meant so much more to her. He was her boyfriend, her closest friend, the one person who shared her passion for helping traumatized horses. Amy visited the hospital almost every day, telling him what was happening on the farm and hoping he would wake up and come back to her. But, so far, there were no signs of any change in his condition.

Amy sighed and pushed away the pain. She had to be strong and keep believing that Ty would recover — it was the only thing she *could* do. She rode to the front yard, where she slipped off Willow's back and ran up the stirrups. As she did so, her older sister, Lou, emerged from one of the stalls, carrying a grooming kit.

"Hi, Amy," she called. "I've just finished grooming Candy."

"Great," said Amy. "How is she?"

"She was a little restless," Lou replied. "But she calmed down after a while. I did some T-touch on her, and that helped. Is there anything else you need me to do before I go in and check the bookings? We had another call today."

Amy smiled. "Go ahead. I can manage, and Ben's already taken care of the feeds. How are the bookings going?"

It was difficult to believe how much bad luck they had suffered at Heartland recently. As well as the storm, there had been an outbreak of equine flu. They hadn't been able to take on any new horses until the vet had given them the all clear, so there were several empty stalls. But in that respect, at least, things were looking up.

"We're getting there," said Lou. "In fact, I got an interesting call this morning, just after you'd gone out. A woman has a wild mustang stallion she's thinking of sending here."

"A mustang!" exclaimed Amy. Her heart leaped. She had read so much about the herds of wild horses that still lived out West. "A completely wild one? He hasn't been gentled at all?"

"He's still wild, from what I could gather," said Lou. "And a stallion. I wasn't sure whether we'd be able to work with him, so I said you'd call her back."

Lou didn't like to make decisions about accepting new patients without consulting Amy. She helped out with the horses, but she wasn't an expert — and she'd grown up in England, so she knew very little about America's wild horses.

Amy's face split into a grin. "Wow, Lou! I'd *love* to work with a mustang! I never thought I'd get the chance. Where's he from? Did she say?"

"Nevada, I think," said Lou, smiling at Amy's enthusiasm. "What makes mustangs so special?"

Amy slipped off Willow's bridle. "Well, they're our national wild horses, for a start," she explained. "They came from Europe originally, but they've been running wild for centuries now. They've had to adapt to life out on the western plains and deserts, so they're really tough. They're survivors."

She lifted the saddle off Willow's back and rested it in the crook of her elbow. "The other thing is that Monty Roberts has done a lot of work with mustangs. His work is amazing. Mom really respected him," she continued, thinking of her mother, who had started treating horses at Heartland. "Monty Roberts is the guy who first developed the join-up technique after watching how horses behave with one another. He realized that the way to gentle horses is to think horse — to speak their language — instead of just beating them into submission."

"Sounds pretty obvious to me," Lou commented.

Amy nodded. "You'd think so," she agreed. "But a lot of people still don't get it. They'll do whatever gives them the fastest results."

She headed toward the tack room. "I'll be in when I've cooled Willow down," she called.

❧

Amy put away Willow's tack and headed back out to the bay pony. She gave her a quick grooming, led her down to one of the paddocks, and turned her out. Then she walked back up to the farmhouse, thinking. *A wild mustang stallion — straight from the deserts of Nevada!* Amy felt a rush of excitement. But at the same time, a host of other thoughts crept in. Amy knew that a mustang arriving in Virginia meant only one thing: There was one less horse roaming free on the plains, and the wild herds continued to shrink.

Amy sighed regretfully. All the wild horses out West were now managed by a single organization called the Bureau of Land Management, or BLM. It was the belief of the BLM that the horses bred too quickly and that their numbers therefore had to be controlled because there was no longer enough open land to support a growing population. The BLM rounded up some of the horses every year and sold them. It sounded fine in theory, but Amy had also read that more and more of the wild lands were being taken over by farmers and real-estate developers and that the mustang herds were gradually shrinking. It was difficult to know what to believe, but she wished that all the wild horses could be left to roam in freedom.

Deep in thought, Amy went indoors and got the mustang owner's number from Lou. *Mrs. Abrahams,* she read, and punched the number into the phone.

"Hello?" said a voice. "Lois Abrahams."

"Hello, Mrs. Abrahams," said Amy. "It's Amy Fleming, from Heartland. I understand you have a mustang you're thinking of sending to us."

"Ah! Yes," said Mrs. Abrahams. "Thank you for calling back. Dazzle's a blue roan stallion. He's very special. I knew he would be from the moment I saw him. I fell in love with him then — just from his picture on the Internet."

She sounded warm and friendly, her voice bubbling over with enthusiasm.

"The Internet?" asked Amy, puzzled. "Didn't you buy him from the Bureau of Land Management?"

"Oh, yes," said Mrs. Abrahams. "They have online auctions to place their horses these days. It's all very up-to-date."

"So anyone can buy a mustang, just like that?" Amy exclaimed with dismay. She didn't mean to be rude, but the idea appalled her. She knew what had happened to mustangs in the past — far too many had ended up being slaughtered for chicken feed when their new owners had found them difficult to train.

"No, no," Mrs. Abrahams replied. "They're very strict. I had to be vetted, and Dazzle won't really be mine until I've shown I can look after him properly for a year."

"I'm glad," said Amy. "I'm relieved to know they are looking out for the future of the horses. How long have you had him?"

"Only a week," said Mrs. Abrahams. "He's really wild, you know! I don't think I'm going to be able to do very much with him until he's had some professional handling. I haven't ridden for years."

Amy contemplated what she had heard. Mrs. Abrahams sounded very pleasant, but she seemed inexperienced for someone taking on a wild horse. "So you're not planning on riding him? You just want to give him a home?" she asked cautiously.

"Oh, no, I hope to ride him eventually," said Mrs. Abrahams confidently. "But I don't think I'm up to training him. That's why I thought of you."

Amy paused, thinking. This was an even bigger challenge than she'd imagined — not only would the mustang need gentling, but he would also need very thorough training to make him safe for a novice rider. "And the Bureau didn't do any work with him before you bought him?" she inquired, checking.

"Only enough to get him from place to place," said Dazzle's owner. "He was tranquilized when he arrived, and he went straight into the paddock. To be honest, I've had problems getting near him since."

"And that's fine with the BLM?"

"Oh, yes. Their main concern is the horse's living conditions. They wanted to know about our paddock and how much space we have," explained Mrs. Abrahams. "He's used to the plains, of course, so he lives outside. If you took him, you'd find that side of things very simple. He just needs a big paddock and a suitable shelter. No extra feeds."

Amy took a deep breath. She looked up and caught Lou's eye. Lou smiled encouragingly, but Amy was hesitant. "He sounds amazing, Mrs. Abrahams. But we'll need to give it some thought. May I call you back?"

"Of course, of course," said Mrs. Abrahams, sounding slightly disappointed. "But I do hope you can take him. I want him to have the best possible start."

Amy put the phone down and sat at the kitchen table, opposite Lou.

"You're not sure?" queried Lou. "I guess it *would* be an undertaking. What was that about the Internet?"

"She bought him through an online auction. I guess it's one of the methods that the BLM uses to find potential buyers," said Amy. "I hadn't heard of it before, though."

"What's this about the BLM?" asked Jack Bartlett, coming through the door. He was Lou and Amy's grandfather and the owner of Heartland.

"We've just been offered the chance to gentle and train a mustang that someone adopted from the Bureau of Land Management," explained Amy. "The owner says she wants to ride him, but he's completely wild. I don't think she has any idea what she's taking on."

"Maybe she does, deep down—and that's why she wants to send him here," suggested Lou.

"I guess so," said Amy. "But if she's as inexperienced as she sounds, we'll have to do a *lot* of work before he can go back to her."

Lou's blue eyes twinkled. "Isn't that just what you want?" she asked gently. "It's not like you to turn down a challenge. There's plenty of room. He wouldn't need a stall, would he?"

Amy shook her head. "No. He'd be much happier outside. We could put him in the bottom paddock, but he'd have to be kept on his own because he's a stallion."

"Well, we've made exceptions for stallions before," Grandpa pointed out.

Amy smiled at them. It was touching to hear Lou and Grandpa persuading her to take on a horse—it was usually the other way around. She wasn't sure why she was hesitating. Mrs. Abrahams clearly needed all the help she could get. And Lou was right — it was an amazing opportunity and surely the best thing for Dazzle in the long run.

She reached for the phone decisively. "We'll take him."

Chapter 2

"That's settled then," said Amy as she hung up the phone. Now that she had made up her mind, the thrill of working with a mustang had returned. "I can't wait to tell Ty. Will you be able to give me a ride to the hospital soon, Lou?"

Lou nodded. "Sure. Half an hour?"

Amy's head was buzzing on the way to the hospital. She missed having Ty around to talk with and to share Heartland's work. They had both learned alongside Amy's mom, Marion, before she died. They had embraced her special understanding of how to approach the horses that came to Heartland.

Although he hadn't shown any response, Amy still made a practice of going to the hospital and sharing everything that happened with Ty. Amy was sure he could hear, and today there was so much to say. She could tell him how well Willow had gone on the ridge and all about Dazzle and the excitement of working with a wild horse.

Lou pulled into the hospital parking lot, and Amy opened her door.

"I'll be back to pick you up in about an hour," said Lou. "Maybe a little sooner. I just need to get a few things in town."

Amy nodded and waved, then headed inside. By now, she knew the route to Ty's bedside blindfolded. Into the elevator, up three floors to Lincoln Ward . . .

She stepped out into the familiar hallway and walked quickly toward Ty's room, humming cheerfully. She swung around the door, a greeting on her lips.

"Hi, Ty."

Amy stopped when she saw that Ty was not alone. There was someone sitting at his bedside. A girl, perhaps a year or two older than Amy, looked up at her. She was pretty, with dark straight hair framing her face.

"Oh, hello," said Amy, startled.

"Hi," said the other girl. She stood up. "Are you here to see Ty, too?"

"Yes," said Amy. She felt confused as she made her way over to Ty's bed. She'd never seen this girl before. She smiled awkwardly. "I'm Amy."

"Pleased to meet you, Amy. I'm Kerry-Ann," said the other girl, sitting down again. "I heard about the storm on the news. I had been out of town that week, but when I got back, some old friends told me that Ty had been injured. I was so upset. I had to come and see him right away."

Amy watched as Kerry-Ann reached out and touched Ty's hand, curling her fingers around his. Amy stared in surprise. She sat down on the other chair. All her thoughts of talking about Dazzle and Willow had gone.

She cleared her throat. "So, you know Ty well?" she managed to ask.

Kerry-Ann nodded. "Oh, yes. You could say that!" she said. "We were in school together. How about you?"

Kerry-Ann seemed so confident, sitting there holding Ty's hand. Amy felt confused, and she flushed slightly. "I'm his girlfriend," she said quietly, "and we work together, too."

"So that's at — Homeland?" ventured Kerry-Ann.

"Heartland," Amy corrected her, with a small smile.

"That's right. I knew I'd heard that somewhere. You work with horses, right?"

Amy nodded and managed to remain quiet, but her head was full of questions. *Who are you?* she wanted to ask. *Why hasn't Ty ever talked about you?* Instead, she turned silently to look at Ty's face. He looked so peaceful. She wondered if he knew they were there. She suddenly had the urge to shake him and wake him up. There were times when his silence drove her crazy. She wanted to hear his voice. She wanted him to tell her how he knew Kerry-Ann. She tried to remember if she'd heard the name before.

Kerry-Ann had fallen silent, but she still was holding on to Ty's hand. Amy wasn't sure what to do with herself. Amy sat motionless for a few more moments, then stood up. "I'd better be going," she said. "I was just stopping by."

Kerry-Ann smiled. If she was feeling awkward, she didn't show it. "Sure. Have a good one," she said. "I'm sure I'll see you again soon."

Amy walked down the hospital corridor slowly, then headed outside and wandered around the grounds to pass the time. *Kerry-Ann. Kerry-Ann.* She was sure she'd never heard that name before. And she certainly hadn't met her. But Kerry-Ann had said she knew Ty well. Amy got the feeling she meant *very* well. It didn't feel right. She'd always felt she knew Ty inside out, and the thought that there were things he'd never told her made Amy uncomfortable. She realized that Ty must have done lots of things — known lots of people — before he'd ever met her. He hadn't started working at Heartland until he was sixteen. She'd just never really thought about it before. Was Kerry-Ann an old girlfriend? Had Ty deliberately avoided mentioning her?

Amy quickly pushed the thought away. She told herself she was jumping to conclusions. *Kerry-Ann's probably just an old friend,* she thought. She sat down on a bench to wait for Lou. She didn't want to doubt Ty, especially not now.

Lou's car drew up, and Amy climbed in.

"You're out early," her sister commented. "How is he?"

Amy shrugged lightly. "Pretty much the same."

Lou shot her a sympathetic glance. "He will wake up, Amy," she said softly.

Amy nodded. "Sure," she replied.

Back at Heartland, Amy found her friend Soraya waiting for her, sitting on the yard gate. She waved and jumped down when Lou's car rolled into the stable yard.

"You're early!" called Amy, smiling as Soraya jogged over.

"Yeah. My mom already had plans with a friend," said Soraya. "So she dropped me off on the way. How's Ty? Your grandpa said you were visiting him. Any improvement?"

Amy shook her head. "No. Nothing new," she said. She hesitated, wondering whether to mention Kerry-Ann. Then she decided against it. She wanted to think about it some more.

"So what can I do?" asked Soraya as they walked toward the farmhouse. "I was going to make a start on cleaning the stalls, but they look pretty clean."

"Yeah, we're caught up with that," said Amy. "We only have twelve horses since the quarantine was just lifted. We're managing with all the stable chores, at least. It's doing the real work that's difficult — treating the horses — especially now that school's started."

Soraya looked sympathetic. "I guess that's where you really miss Ty," she remarked.

Amy nodded. There wasn't anyone else at Heartland who could replace the work that Ty did. But there was no point in dwelling on it. "I thought we could do some work with Blackjack in his stall," she said. "You can help me with that. He basically needs lots of attention — grooming and love. He was taken for granted, so we want to rebuild his trust. But first, I need some lunch. I'm starving. Do you want a sandwich?"

"Oh, I had lunch ages ago," said Soraya. "You go ahead. I'll grab a grooming kit and get started."

"Great," said Amy. "He's in the back barn."

"OK," said Soraya. "See you soon."

In the kitchen, Amy quickly spread mustard on some slices of bread and rummaged in the fridge for some ham, thinking about Soraya's words. She missed Ty more than anyone could guess. She had always believed that their friendship was special, even before they'd started dating. They spent so much time together, she didn't think they had any secrets. But the thought of Kerry-Ann sitting by his bed just wouldn't go away.

Frustrated, she slammed the fridge door and hurriedly slapped her sandwich together. She ate it quickly on her way back down to the yard, forcing herself to focus on Blackjack. ·

"He's doing so much better," commented Soraya when Amy arrived at his stall. Soraya was grooming the horse's neck in smooth, rhythmic strokes with a body brush. "He hasn't snapped at me once. In fact, I think he's enjoying himself. Aren't you, boy?"

Amy smiled and let herself into the stall. It was true — Blackjack was doing well. His owners had sent him to Heartland because, after years of good behavior in their riding school, he had started getting more and more belligerent. His temper had become a real problem. He was a nightmare to catch, and he lashed out constantly in his stall, both with his feet and his teeth.

Amy had gradually realized that, as sometimes happens with riding school horses, he had grown bored and resentful. He was fourteen now and had seen many hard years of plodding around a training ring. Amy couldn't blame him for becoming grouchy! But with the attention and praise of everyone at Heartland, his behavior was gradually improving. Amy had also been giving him the willow Bach Flower Remedy, an herbal extract that would help him feel less resentful and more receptive to the work she was doing with him. He was beginning to seem like a different horse.

Amy stroked the gelding's forelock out of his eyes and fished in her pocket for a handful of pony nuts. "There you go, boy," she said as he nosed her palm with his soft lips. Then she scratched his forehead and behind his ears.

"He's just lapping it up," said Soraya, brushing along his back with smooth sweeps. "I might leave his hind legs to you, though — if you don't mind."

"Sure thing," said Amy, smiling. "But he's quite gentle now."

They worked in silence for a few minutes, absorbed in the rhythm of it. Then the barn door opened, and Amy looked up. Ben, a Heartland stable hand, came and leaned over the stall door.

"Hi, you guys," he greeted them, flashing a grin at Soraya.

"Oh, hi, Ben," Soraya said, briefly glancing up from her work.

Amy looked at her friend in surprise. Soraya usually made a fuss over Ben, but today she seemed rather distracted. Amy smiled at him. "How's Red doing?" she asked.

"Getting better all the time," he said. "He's about three-quarters fit, I'd say."

Red had been one of the horses to suffer from the equine flu that had spread through the stable a few weeks earlier. Red was Ben's own horse, a talented jumper, and the illness had taken him right off the show circuit. But Ben had been careful not to push him too hard while retraining — he cared about him too much for that. "I was wondering if there's anything you wanted me to do, Amy," he continued. "I was hoping to fit in a session with Red this afternoon."

"Go ahead," said Amy. "If you've got time when you're done, you could maybe lunge Silver, but only gently. She needs loosening up. She shouldn't need more than fifteen minutes or so. Oh — I do have some news. We've got a wild mustang arriving tomorrow!"

Soraya and Ben looked at her in astonishment. "What — for training?" asked Ben, openmouthed.

Amy nodded. "His new owner wants us to gentle him. He's a stallion, fresh from the plains of Nevada."

"That's fantastic!" breathed Soraya. "How exciting!"

Amy grinned. After the awkward encounter with Kerry-Ann, she'd forgotten how pleased she was about Dazzle. But the excitement was now welling up again. "I know," she said. "It's an amazing opportunity. I can't wait."

"When will he be arriving?" asked Ben.

"Sometime in the morning," said Amy. "Do you think you'll be around? I might need some help."

"You bet I'll be here," said Ben. "Well, I'd better get going. See you, Soraya."

"Yeah. See you," said Soraya as she and Amy watched Ben head out of the barn.

When he'd gone, Amy turned to her friend. "You were very . . . casual with Ben," she commented, probing gently.

Soraya blushed slightly and brushed Blackjack's side more slowly. "I didn't think you'd notice," she said awkwardly.

"Come on! It was obvious!" Amy told her. "You are usually so interested in Ben and Red. Is everything OK?"

"Yes! Everything's fine. Nothing's happened. Well — nothing with Ben. It's just that I was thinking about . . . something else."

Amy studied her friend's face. Soraya's mouth was creased with a coy smile, and Amy was intrigued. She'd had a crush on Ben for so long. "Some*one* else, you mean?" she quizzed. "Soraya, you can tell me!"

Soraya swallowed. "Yes, I know," she whispered. "Amy, you have to promise you won't tell anyone."

"As if I would!" exclaimed Amy. She thought rapidly as she moved around Blackjack's side and started brush-

ing his hind legs. *Who could make Soraya feel like this —
and make her be embarrassed about it?* Amy knew her friend
well, and she assumed there weren't that many options.
"Soraya, it's not Matt, is it?"

Matt was one of their friends from school — they'd
both known him for years. This semester, Matt and
Soraya had the leads in the school's production of *Romeo
and Juliet.*

Soraya's eyes opened wide. "Amy! How did you
guess?" she said with a gasp.

Amy laughed. "I used my best deductive reasoning."

"It's just that we've been spending so much time together," explained Soraya. "Ever since play practice
started, we've been talking a lot after rehearsals and
stuff." She stopped. "You don't mind, do you?" she
asked.

"Mind? Why would I mind?" Amy exclaimed, aston-
ished. Matt had once been interested in going out with
Amy, but that was ancient history. It seemed so long ago.
"It would be great if two of my closest friends went out."

The color of Soraya's cheeks deepened as she shook
her head. "Slow down, Amy," she said. "I don't think
he's interested in me that way," she added wistfully.

"Well, I don't see why not," said Amy. "I think you'd
make a great pair."

It was true. Her two friends were really well-suited.

Why hadn't she seen it before? She smiled at the idea of it. But then, in spite of herself, a wave of loneliness washed over her. She thought of Ty, lying in the hospital. She bent down and leaned against one of Blackjack's legs. She gently lifted his hoof and proceeded to pick it in silence.

Chapter Three

❧

"Amy! There's a trailer coming up the driveway," Lou shouted up the stairs.

"I'm coming!" called Amy, pulling on a pair of jeans. Running around trying to get everything ready for Dazzle, she had accidentally bumped into Ben with a bucket of water on the yard, and she'd been soaked. The October mornings were getting chilly, so she'd dashed inside to change into something dry.

She ran down the stairs and out the door. The trailer had pulled up, and a couple were climbing down from the cab. They were in their forties, and both looked easygoing and friendly.

"Mrs. Abrahams?" asked Amy, stepping forward.

"That's right. You must be Amy," said the woman, shaking her hand. "Nice to meet you."

As she said this, there was a thunder of hooves from inside the trailer. Mrs. Abrahams glanced around anxiously.

"He's pretty restless," she said. "It's been difficult for him. We had a terrible time loading him. We had to call the neighbors to help. Maybe it's best if we get him out right away."

"Of course," Amy agreed.

Grandpa, Ben, and Lou stood by as Amy and Mrs. Abrahams undid the bolts on the trailer. Mr. Abrahams went to hold on to Dazzle's lead rope from the inside. As the ramp creaked open, stamping and whinnying reverberated from within the trailer.

With a fury of defiance, Dazzle stormed out of the trailer. It was clear that Mr. Abrahams had little control. Amy gasped at the sheer power and beauty of the horse. He was fired up with desire to be out of the trailer and, seeing the sea of human faces, the stallion screamed and reared. He seemed to linger in the air, his hooves flailing dangerously close to Mrs. Abrahams's head.

Ben dashed forward and grabbed the stallion's halter as the lead slipped from Mr. Abrahams's grasp. Amy quickly reached up to help Ben. Together they grappled with the overexcited horse.

"Let's try to get him right down to the paddock," suggested Amy, and with a concerted effort, she, Ben, and Mr. Abrahams led the stallion forward. It was a battle every inch of the way. All the mustang's strength was pitched against them in a fierce struggle to break free.

Grandpa jogged on ahead to open the paddock gate, and eventually they made it. Mr. Abrahams quickly unclipped the lead rope, and they all watched as Dazzle thundered off, his head held low, another piercing scream filling the air. He tore around the far corner of the paddock, looking for an escape route in the fencing. Amy's heart thudded fast — this horse wasn't used to being contained, not even in a large and grassy paddock. He was used to the open range — to freedom.

"Well, at least he hasn't tried jumping," said Grandpa, a note of relief in his voice as he watched the horse gallop around the pasture's perimeter. "If he does, I think the fences should be high enough to keep him in here."

"Yes, he should be fine," Mr. Abrahams assured them. "He didn't get over our fences, and they're about the height of these. I imagine he'll settle down after a day or two — but he's always on the hunt for a way out."

The group turned and walked back up to the yard. Amy looked back at the beautiful blue roan stallion that stood watching them for an instant, his tail held high. He whipped around, then bucked and cantered at the fences once more, searching for his freedom. His energy and anger took Amy's breath away. *It's going to be fantastic to connect with him!* she thought. She shook her head in awe, then jogged to catch up with the others.

In the farmhouse kitchen, the Abrahamses explained how they had come to adopt Dazzle from the BLM.

"We went out West on vacation last year," explained Mrs. Abrahams. "We started in Vegas, then drove farther north. That's when we saw the herds of wild horses. I have always been a horse person, and I fell in love with them right away. I was so shocked when I found out that some people consider them to be a nuisance. To me, they are a symbol of our country's heritage, the untamed nature of the West. When we came back, I decided to read about them a little more."

Amy listened, fascinated. However inexperienced she might be, Mrs. Abrahams clearly felt passionately about the plight of the wild horses.

"I found out that these horses are really under threat," Mrs. Abrahams continued. "The Bureau of Land Management keeps a close eye on the herds, and rounds a few up whenever their numbers get out of control. I didn't really see the need — there's so much space out West, but people want more land all the time. So, anyway, I figured the least I could do was take one of them on."

Amy nodded. Mrs. Abrahams's explanation matched what Amy had read herself. "So have you ever owned a horse before?" she asked. "You said you haven't ridden for a while."

"I used to have a riding horse, but we sold him when

we had the kids," said Mrs. Abrahams. "Though, like I said on the phone, I don't think that really matters to the BLM. As long as you mean well and have the right facilities, they're happy to let you try. But they retain ownership for a year. If things aren't working out after that, they take back the horse. That keeps people from buying them cheap and then immediately selling them," she finished.

Now that she'd met her, Amy felt much better about Mrs. Abrahams's intentions. And Dazzle had already captured her own heart. Horses could gain so much from developing a close bond with people, as long as it was established with understanding and care — and that was what Amy would give Dazzle. Whatever he may have left behind, she would do her utmost to see that the stallion had a bright future.

"Well, we're so pleased you've brought him here," Amy said warmly. "I'm looking forward to working with him."

"You'll let me know how it's going?" asked Mrs. Abrahams.

"Of course," Amy reassured her. "And feel free to drop by anytime to see for yourself."

After the Abrahamses had gone, Amy walked back down to the bottom paddock. She had filled a bucket with water and had added a few drops of Bach's Rescue

Remedy. She hoped it would calm down the stallion and help him adjust to his new surroundings.

Slowly, she let herself through the gate. On seeing her, Dazzle threw up his head and bolted around the paddock. It distressed Amy to see him so panicked, so intractable. She stood still, waiting for him to calm down. At last, he slowed to a trot and stared at her. Tentatively, she took a step toward him. He immediately reared up and galloped away from her once more.

Amy stepped back. He was clearly too wound up to let her get any closer. She put down the bucket, hoping he'd drink from it if she left him on his own. She left the paddock knowing there was little more she could do for the time being.

❧

Forcing herself to refocus, Amy went to another paddock and caught Candy, a talented strawberry roan mare. She had been sent to Heartland because she had started to pull at the bit and sidestep, especially at shows. Candy had also caught the equine flu, so Amy had been working with her gently as she regained her strength. Amy still had not been able to determine exactly what was troubling the mare and causing her to act up.

Amy led Candy up to the stable, tacked her up, then rode her down to the training ring. As they neared the bottom paddock, Dazzle's shrill whinny made Candy stop in her tracks. She whinnied a call in return, her ears pricked forward eagerly.

"Come on, girl," murmured Amy, pushing her forward again.

Candy tensed as she fought to hold her ground. As Dazzle called again, Candy resisted Amy with determination, tossing her head against the bit and backing up. Amy sat deep in the saddle, shortened her reins, and drove the mare on. Eventually, Candy reluctantly moved forward, sidestepping and dancing as she did so. Amy wasn't surprised. Stallions could even have an unsettling effect on levelheaded mares — and Candy was more unpredictable than most.

She rode the mare in circles and figure eights around the ring. Candy soon settled down and began to move well, accepting the bit and bending at Amy's cue. She was a joy to ride when she was like this. Amy could ask her to collect her stride with delicate articulation, then just as smoothly extend it again, and then extend it farther so that her long, graceful strides ate up the ground beneath them.

Not wanting to overstretch her, Amy soon brought Candy to a walk and rode her back up to the yard. There hadn't been any signs of her bad behavior during the workout, and Amy was still mystified as to what the mare's underlying problem might be.

After cooling Candy and turning her out again, Amy

returned to Dazzle's pasture to check the bucket of water. It looked untouched. The stallion glowered at her from the far end of the paddock. Deciding not to force the issue, Amy returned to the gate and leaned on it, watching him. He was so tough and wiry, his muscles finely honed from the demanding life on the desert plains. She hadn't seen him graze once, in spite of the inviting green grass. It was a sure sign that he was stressed. She sighed with uncertainty and headed to the farmhouse.

❧

Everyone was too busy to sit around the Sunday lunch table for long. Lou had agreed to drive Amy to the hospital for an early afternoon visit.

"D'you mind getting the bus back?" asked Lou. "I'd like to see Scott later — I feel like I haven't seen him in weeks."

Scott was the local equine vet and Lou's boyfriend. Over the years, he had spent so much time with the horses at Heartland that he was almost part of the family; but he was very busy with his other clients as well. It was sometimes difficult for Scott and Lou to coordinate their hectic schedules.

"Sure, no problem," said Amy. "I'm ready to go when you are."

As they headed down the driveway, Amy realized that she hadn't given much thought to Kerry-Ann since her last hospital visit. She'd been too preoccupied with the horses, especially Dazzle. Now she hoped that she'd have the chance to be alone with Ty for a while. Surely Kerry-Ann wouldn't be visiting every day?

At the hospital, Amy waved good-bye to Lou and headed inside. Mrs. Baldwin, Ty's mom, was coming out of the elevator as Amy approached it.

"Hi, Mrs. Baldwin," Amy greeted her, smiling. They had hardly known each other prior to Ty's accident, but they had grown closer since they had both been spending so much time at the hospital. Amy was now very fond of Mrs. Baldwin and appreciated her support.

"Amy! Good to see you. I'm just on my way to work."

"Work?" queried Amy. Amy knew that Mrs. Baldwin had been depressed for a long time. She had a tendency to remain sequestered in her house, relying on Ty and his father to do the shopping and other errands. As far as Amy knew, she hadn't had a job for years.

Mrs. Baldwin beamed. "I got a job in a local retirement home. It's what I used to do, before . . . " She trailed off.

Amy broke in quickly to cover Mrs. Baldwin's embarrassment. "That's great," she said warmly. "I'm so pleased."

"Yes. Well, Ty's accident has really forced me to look at things differently. I need to get out there again. It's been a long time since I've been able to be a part of something — to contribute," said Mrs. Baldwin earnestly. "Of course, I've got a lot to learn. So much has changed since my last job. But it's all good experience for when Ty starts recovering and comes home."

It was good to hear the conviction in Mrs. Baldwin's voice. Not *if* Ty came home, *when* he came home. Amy smiled. "I hope it's soon," she said.

Mrs. Baldwin nodded. "I do, too. Well, I'd best be going. See you soon, Amy."

Amy could hardly believe the change in Mrs. Baldwin. She was so positive now and so full of energy. *Ty would be so proud of her,* she thought.

Amy stepped out of the elevator and walked down the hallway. There was a nurse ahead of her, carrying a large bouquet of flowers. The nurse turned into Ty's room, and Amy slowed down slightly as she reached the doorway. She could hear the nurse talking to someone. Curious, she peeked in, wondering who the other visitor might be. Recognizing the profile, Amy took a step back. It was Ty's dad. As the nurse arranged the flowers by the bedside, Amy could see that Brad Baldwin was talking to his son. Amy felt reluctant to interrupt. Unlike Ty's mother, Mr. Baldwin had never warmed to her. He had always resented the fact that Ty worked with horses, and he had made no secret of it. So Amy lingered outside the doorway, hesitating.

She didn't mean to eavesdrop, but in spite of herself, she could overhear what the man was saying. "Someone's sent you some flowers, son," she heard. "Let's see who it is."

Amy heard the envelope being opened. "Ah," Brad said. His voice was gruff, but he sounded pleased. "They're from that girl you used to go with at school."

Amy's heart leaped into her throat, and she held her breath. She was craning to hear every word now.

Brad was reading the card aloud. "'To Ty, hope you're out of there real soon. I'll be here when you wake up! Love from Kerry-Ann.'" There was a pause, then Brad sighed. "You remember Kerry-Ann, don't you? She was such a nice, sensible girl — not into all the horse nonsense."

Amy's heart thudded. She swallowed. She'd never heard Ty's father sounding so wistful about anything! It seemed to contradict his harsh, cynical nature.

She quickly peeked into the room again. She could just see Brad, sitting in the chair closest to Ty's bed, leaning forward with his elbows on his knees. He was holding a little greeting card in his large, callused hands. She leaned back against the wall and let out her breath.

So Kerry-Ann hadn't just been a friend. She'd been a

girlfriend. Well, she'd suspected that from the start. And what was more, Ty's father had clearly approved of Kerry-Ann — and liked her. Amy wished he could feel the same way about her. She felt tears threatening and quickly retraced her steps down the corridor. She couldn't face Mr. Baldwin. Not now . . .

Chapter Four

Amy slipped into a waiting room at the end of the hallway and stood where she'd be able to see Ty's father
leaving. He didn't stay much longer. After ten minutes
or so, she saw Brad walk up to the elevator, his hands in
his pockets and his head down.

When she was sure he had gone, Amy almost ran to
Ty's room. She snatched up the card. It was a get well
card with a picture of a dog holding up a bandaged paw
on the front. She read the message inside. It was just as
Brad had read aloud — there was nothing more. She
hurriedly put down the card as Dr. Reubens came in to
check on his patient. She felt a rush of guilt when she
looked up and realized that she hadn't even said hello to
Ty yet. She watched as the doctor examined him.

"Have there been any changes at all?" Amy asked.

"Not so far," the doctor replied sympathetically. "But that doesn't mean he won't come around. He could wake up at any time. Although, keep in mind that once he does, it will be a while before he's back to his old self. Temporary memory loss is common in postcoma patients. His recovery, both mental and physical, will take time."

"You mean Ty might not remember anything . . . or anyone?" Amy queried, trying to hide her anxiety.

"Well, that's one possibility. More often, though, the memory loss is selective, so he may recall certain things but not others. It's usually a temporary condition, but in some cases it can be permanent. It's impossible to say for certain — everyone's different. We'll just have to wait and see."

The doctor finished his work and left the room. Amy sat still for a while, deep in thought. She knew it was possible that Ty might not wake up, but right now she could only think about what would happen if he did come out of his coma but didn't remember her or Heartland. For nearly three years, Ty had been dedicated to Heartland and the horses there. What if, when he came to, all those memories were gone?

Amy impulsively reached out and grabbed Ty's hand, trying to push away the image of Kerry-Ann doing the same thing the last time Amy had visited. She leaned forward. "Ty," she whispered. "Can you hear me? Ty," she said again. "Ty, it's Amy. I need you. Heartland needs you and I hope you haven't forgotten us. There's so much I want to talk to you about."

But then, somehow, she couldn't find words for what she wanted to say. She was tempted to mention Kerry-Ann, but her pride wouldn't let her. And when she thought about all the news she had been looking forward to sharing with Ty, she found she didn't have the heart to tell him about Dazzle — or even to say how proud she was of his mom. So she sat in silence, holding Ty's hand until a nurse came in to change his position.

Amy then decided to head home. She stood up, smiled at the nurse, and slipped out the door.

❧

Scott's pickup was in the driveway when Amy got back to Heartland. Amy remembered that he had plans with Lou. She went into the farmhouse and found the two of them together, poring over the local newspaper at the kitchen table.

"Hi, Amy," Scott greeted her. "How's Ty?"

"Just the same," said Amy flatly. She went to the fridge and poured herself a glass of apple juice. "How are things?"

"Fine, thanks," said Scott. "The usual. Busy."

"Amy," said Lou, looking up from the newspaper, "do you know someone named Nancy?"

Amy frowned. "Nancy? I don't think so. Why?"

"She called just after I got back. She was asking for Grandpa. There was just something in the way she spoke — like she knew Grandpa really well. But I've never heard him mention her. I just wondered if you and Mom might have known her before I came back to Heartland."

Amy thought for a minute. "I don't think so," she said. "Doesn't ring any bells."

"OK. I'll just tell Grandpa when he comes in," said Lou.

"I heard that," said Grandpa as he opened the door. He stepped into the kitchen and took off his hat, wiping his brow with his forearm. "Tell me what?" he asked.

"That a certain someone named Nancy called for you," Lou taunted.

Much to Amy's astonishment, Grandpa's face broke into a beaming smile. He even turned slightly pink.

"Did she now!" he exclaimed.

Lou grinned at him. "Grandpa! Who is she?" she asked with a laugh.

Grandpa shook his head, smiling. "Now don't go jumping to conclusions," he said. "I knew Nancy Marshall years ago. She lived with her husband on a farm, on the other side of Clairdale Ridge. When he died, she went back to her family up in New England."

"So she's back here visiting?" asked Lou.

"No. It seems she's decided to take up farming again. She's got a place over toward Clairdale, not far from where she was before. I bumped into her at the hardware store the other day. Quite a coincidence, really. I was looking at fencing, and so was she. I didn't even recognize her at first. Then we got chatting, and suddenly it all came flooding back."

"Well, I don't think it was a fence she was calling about," said Lou, raising one eyebrow comically. "I left her number by the phone."

Grandpa laughed heartily. He took off his coat, chuckling, and went to the office.

"Isn't that nice?" commented Lou to Amy when he was out of earshot. "Grandpa's been on his own for so long. Wouldn't it be great if he found someone?"

Amy smiled and nodded. "Yeah. He deserves it," she agreed, heading outside again. But inside, she suddenly felt very much alone.

Out on the yard, Amy took a deep breath. She *was* happy for Grandpa — of course she was. Yet, somehow, seeing Lou and Scott together and thinking about her grandfather dating again made her feel lonely. It made her miss Ty even more.

The afternoon was wearing on. Amy decided to take Blackjack out on a trail ride. It would be good for him, and it would help her to clear her thoughts. She hurried to the tack room, then to Blackjack's stall.

His whinny greeted her as soon as she entered the barn, and Amy's heart lifted slightly. The gelding was getting more attached to her every day, and he was regaining his trust in people. He was another Heartland success. She smiled as she entered his stall.

"Hello there, Blackjack," she whispered. "We're going out on the trails together. You'll like that, won't you, boy?"

She stroked his soft muzzle for a moment, and he nuzzled her affectionately. Then she tacked him up quickly and led him out. The afternoon air had a chill, and she pushed the gelding into a brisk trot as they set off up the trail leading toward Teak's Hill. It felt good to get away from everything, even just for an hour.

But as she rode, questions surged through Amy's mind. She'd never been consumed by such doubt and uncertainty, especially not about Ty. Was she just jealous of Kerry-Ann, or was it something more? She thought of Ty's father talking about the "horse nonsense." Of course, she'd always known that Ty's dad hated that he worked with horses, but she'd never really witnessed it before. Not like this. Now she realized his father must have been saying things like that for years. Amy could only imagine what Mr. Baldwin thought now. He probably blamed Heartland for the accident. And what if, when Ty woke up, he felt the same as his dad?

Amy urged Blackjack into a canter, pushing the thoughts away. The gelding responded willingly, lengthening his stride and gliding over the ground. They reached the fallen tree trunks and turned toward them. Blackjack pricked his ears forward and popped over the jumps, flicking his tail as he landed. In spite of herself, Amy smiled happily at the horse's playfulness and clapped his neck. She thought of all the years that the gelding must have been ridden carelessly, being pushed and pulled around. Coming to Heartland had been a tonic for him, but Amy was concerned about what would happen when he went back to his owners. She'd have to make sure they understood the care and attention that he needed in the future.

Dusk was drawing in as they clattered back into the yard. Amy untacked Blackjack and gave him a rubdown in his stall. When she'd finished, she didn't feel like going inside yet, so instead she headed down to the bottom paddock to check on Dazzle. She approached quietly and was relieved to see him grazing with quick, hungry snatches. He'd calmed down that much, at least.

He heard her approach and flung up his head, his nostrils flaring. Amy stood still, and they stared at each other in the fading light. She moved a step closer. Dazzle instantly pivoted on his hind legs and wheeled around. Once he was at the far end of the paddock, he stopped and turned to face her again.

Amy didn't try to approach. She had realized that all she could do was place herself in his presence until he began to accept her. The stallion stood rigid for several minutes, eyeing her nervously. Then he turned and cantered along the length of the far fence, hunting for an exit once more.

Amy watched him, feeling frustrated. She longed to make contact with the fiery stallion and gain his trust. But it was clearly going to take a lot of time and patience.

Chapter Five

Amy's alarm shrilled in her ears, pulling her out of a deep, dreamless sleep. She reached out to silence it and stayed huddled under her duvet for a few moments, steeling herself to get out of bed and face the cold gray morning. She didn't feel like getting up — everything seemed to involve so much effort and offered so little hope in return. She had really tried to be positive about Ty and to convince herself that he would soon return. But nothing had changed. Not a thing.

And nothing had changed with Dazzle, either. He was showing no sign of responding to her, and Amy was beginning to question how she would make any progress if she couldn't even get near him.

She forced herself up and dressed quickly, then ran

down the stairs. She wondered how Dazzle had been overnight and hurried to the bottom pasture to see him.

She spotted him in the first light of dawn, standing with one hind leg resting, his head drooping as he dozed. It was the first time she'd seen him at ease, but he was aware of her presence in an instant and catapulted into life, retreating to the depths of the pasture. Amy opened the gate and went over to his bucket. The stallion had still hardly touched the water.

Amy sighed. It was no use hoping that herbal remedies would help if he wouldn't even sniff them.

She took the bucket back to the yard and started on the morning chores. By the time she'd mucked out three of the stalls, Ben had arrived.

"Hi, Amy!" he called across the yard, getting out of his pickup. "How are things? Any progress with Dazzle?"

Amy put down the wheelbarrow she was using and pushed a strand of hair out of her eyes. She shook her head. "He's still completely distant," she admitted. "He isn't interested in anything other than finding a way out."

"He's some horse," said Ben. "I want to go and take another look at him later, but should I take over the mucking for now? Then you can feed everyone."

"Yeah, thanks," said Amy. They had developed a good system between them over the last few weeks, but things would soon get harder. With the October evenings drawing in, more of the horses would need stabling, which meant more work all around. Now that only Amy was working directly with the horses, Ben did as much of the stable work as he could, and Lou helped, too. Even with the three of them, it was a lot to manage.

Amy handed the wheelbarrow to Ben and went into the feed room. She looked at her watch — almost seven-thirty. She was running late. Hurriedly, she lined up the feed buckets and began distributing them. By the time she'd finished, it was almost eight, and she barely had time to take a shower and throw on her school clothes. Running down the Heartland driveway, she realized she'd forgotten to do her history homework. Too late! She'd have to do it at break.

"Hi, Amy!" called Soraya as Amy scrambled onto the bus just in time. "You're out of breath!"

"Yeah. What's new?" gasped Amy, flopping onto the seat beside her. "There's just never enough time."

"So, how's Dazzle?" asked Soraya.

Amy sighed. "I don't have much of an update. Absolutely zero progress. I think he has the most independent spirit I've ever come across," she said. She smiled wryly. "It's pretty magnificent."

"You'll feel so accomplished when you reach him," Soraya enthused.

Amy nodded thoughtfully. "That's an understatement," she said. "I just hope it works out."

"It usually does," Soraya reassured her warmly. "I've never known you to fail, Amy."

"Thanks for that," Amy replied, touched by her friend's praise.

The bus stopped, and Matt got on. He strolled nonchalantly to the seat in front of them and sat down. "Hey," he said lightly.

"Hi, Matt," said Amy, noticing that Soraya had flushed slightly. "How was your weekend?"

"Nothing special. I've been trying to learn my lines," he said, flashing a quick look at Soraya. Amy saw their eyes meet, just for an instant, then slide away again.

"Oh, right. I learned some, too," said Soraya, a little self-consciously. "But it takes forever, doesn't it? I think I've memorized them, then half an hour later my mind's a blank."

Matt grinned. "Yeah. I keep trying things like putting them under my pillow so I can absorb them during my sleep. No luck."

Soraya giggled. "I tried sticking a page to the bathroom mirror, but it got soaked."

Amy listened to their easy banter and smiled to herself. They would make a good pair if they got together. Then her thoughts drifted to Ty. Their relationship was far from typical. They had never done the things that most couples their age did, like go to plays or movies or into town. Their whole relationship had revolved around Heartland and helping the horses. She'd never known anything else. She'd never *wanted* anything else.

But Ty had. He'd suggested they go on a date — a real date — but Amy had always been too busy. Maybe he'd gone to the movies with Kerry-Ann, and to get ice cream. They might have been a real couple. Amy felt a pang of anxiety. The more she thought about it, she was certain she'd let him down.

Then she shook herself, knowing she couldn't change anything now. When Ty came out of his coma, things would be different. She'd make all the time in the world for him.

At break, Amy fished out her history book and sat down in homeroom to do her homework. Soraya and Matt sat with her, laughing together and coming up with suggestions.

"You two aren't helping," groaned Amy, trying to concentrate.

"Here, let me take a look," said Matt, quickly scanning her work. "You're almost there. You just need a concluding paragraph."

"Enjoying your little harem, are you, Matt?" drawled a voice. They all looked up, knowing what to expect. A blond girl stood there, eyeing them with disdain.

Matt sighed and ran a hand through his hair. "Hi, Ashley," he said warily. "How's it going?"

"Oh, I'm fine," said Ashley. She turned to Amy. "I see you still haven't come to your senses, Amy. Why are you wasting that horse of yours on Daniel Lawson?"

"Excuse me?" exclaimed Amy. She had recently sold her show jumper, Storm, to a well-respected and successful stable. She'd had to make a painful choice between committing herself to Heartland and competing regularly on Storm. She had concluded that Heartland came first. Storm's new rider, Daniel, was a good friend of Amy's. Most important, Amy knew that her horse was happy.

"You'll regret it in the end," Ashley carried on. "Storm would have done much better at Green Briar."

Amy snorted. "I don't think so, Ashley," she said. Amy was confident she had made the right decision.

Ashley's mother, Val Grant, was the owner of Green Briar, a successful stable that prided itself on winning ribbons. Green Briar had countless trainers and riders who would do whatever was necessary to reach its goals.

"Well, Matt's coming to see me and Bright Magic beat Storm this weekend," simpered Ashley. "Aren't you, Matt?"

"Am I?" said Matt, looking baffled.

"You promised," said Ashley in a huff. "Don't try and pretend you didn't."

Matt spread his hands and shrugged. "It's news to me, Ashley," he said, sounding slightly annoyed.

Ashley stood up, then bent down close to his ear. "We'll figure out the details later," she said softly, but loud enough for Soraya and Amy to hear.

They watched her saunter off. Matt shook his head in disbelief. "She's crazy," he said. "I can't believe I actually *dated* her."

Amy and Soraya exchanged glances and suppressed their smiles. *Neither can we,* thought Amy.

"She can't believe you actually broke up with her," said Amy.

"Well, I did. It's over," said Matt hurriedly, with a quick look at Soraya. "Dead and buried."

✥

Soraya stayed after school to practice her role as Juliet with the girl who was playing the nurse, so Amy took the bus home with Matt.

"I can always count on Ashley to stir up trouble," she commented as the bus rumbled out of the school parking lot. "She made me remember how much I miss Storm."

"Are you getting to see him much?" asked Matt.

Amy shook her head. "There's just too much going on

at Heartland. We can't get all the work done — not without Ty."

"Yeah," said Matt sympathetically. "That's what Soraya was saying the other day. I'm sorry, Amy. I can't believe what you're going through."

Amy shrugged. "Hey, that's OK. We're coping." Then she smiled. "You and Soraya seem to be entrenched in *Romeo and Juliet*."

Matt grinned. "Yeah. I signed up because I needed some extra credit in English. But I really like it. Who would have thought I could act?" He hesitated. "You know, Amy . . . " He stopped quickly and looked around the bus. "Can I tell you something?"

"Sure," said Amy. Just looking at his face, she had a feeling she knew what was coming. "Anything."

"It's just that — I've been spending more time with Soraya. I . . . I think I really like her," said Matt in a rush. He sighed. "But we've been friends for such a long time. I don't think she sees me as more than that. I don't know what to do about it."

Amy smiled at him. "It's not like you to hold back, Matt," she said teasingly.

Matt smiled bashfully. "I guess not. But somehow it feels different with Soraya. I don't want to mess things up."

Amy thought for a moment. She wondered whether to tell him what she knew but decided it wasn't really up to her. It would be much better for Matt and Soraya to talk to each other about their feelings.

"Like you say, you and Soraya go back a long way," she said carefully. "Why not try talking to her? She won't judge you for it. She knows you too well."

Matt let out his breath slowly. "D'you really think that's what I should do?"

Amy nodded. "Yeah." She punched him playfully. "Go for it!"

Amy was smiling to herself about Matt and Soraya as she made her way up the farmhouse steps. She opened the door and said hello to Lou, who was peeling potatoes for supper and seemed slightly preoccupied.

"Any news?" Amy asked, helping herself to a couple of cookies.

"Mrs. Abrahams called to see how Dazzle's doing," said Lou. "I wasn't sure what to tell her, so I said he was still restless and you were just getting to know him at the moment. Hope that's OK. Ben spent some time in the paddock, but he didn't get near him." She turned around from the sink and faced Amy. "You know, I've been thinking. We're running a rescue stable and the only person who can actually work with the horses is at school all day."

Amy felt slightly taken aback. "You think I don't know that?" she asked.

"Of course you do," said Lou. "But there's so much for you to do. The horses are barely getting enough exercise, let alone proper treatment. And now you have a completely wild mustang to deal with!"

"I'm doing my best," said Amy somewhat defensively.

Lou smiled. "Sorry, Amy, I'm not trying to pick a fight with you. This is harder for you than anyone — I know that. That's just the point. I've been trying to think of ways to make it easier for you."

Amy shrugged. "The only thing I can think of is leaving all the chores to you and Ben, and that's not fair. You know it's not."

Lou looked at Amy frankly. "*Your* work is what counts, Amy. No one else can do it. If that's what it takes, that's what we'll have to do."

Amy thought about it. "It would mean I could work with a horse in the morning," she said slowly. "And two in the evening."

"And that would be an improvement, wouldn't it?" said Lou, smiling.

Amy nodded. It still didn't feel quite right, but she knew her sister's idea made sense.

"Well, that's settled then," said Lou firmly. "We'll talk to Ben."

"OK. Thanks, Lou," said Amy, relieved that Lou was taking care of it. "I'm going to do some work with Dazzle now. I'll just get changed."

As she turned toward the stairs, Lou called after her. "Oh, I forgot," she called. "Daniel wanted you to know that Storm won at Staywell on Saturday."

"Thanks, that's great!" exclaimed Amy from halfway up the stairs. She thought of Ashley's words earlier that day. It was good to know that Storm was doing well — not that Amy had any doubt.

"Yeah," added Lou. "He said it was close, but Storm pulled through in the clutch."

Amy grinned. "Thanks for letting me know. I'll give him a call later."

She leaped up the remaining stairs and pulled on her work jeans, thinking about Storm and Dazzle. They were both magnificent horses but so different. Storm was well behaved, well trained, and obedient. Dazzle was at the opposite end of the spectrum — pure spirit, untouched by human interaction. *Which was better?* wondered Amy. She couldn't be sure.

❧

Amy walked briskly down to Dazzle's paddock and bumped into Ben, who was riding Red up from the training ring.

"Hi!" called Amy.

"Hi," Ben responded. "Are you on your way to see Dazzle?"

Amy nodded. "Lou told me you checked on him today."

"Yeah. I didn't try anything with him, though. Thought I'd leave it to the expert," said Ben with a smile. "It's fantastic just to watch him. When he doesn't realize you are there, his movements are so free. D'you mind waiting for me while I put Red away? I'd like to see you work with him."

"Sure," said Amy. "But I have to warn you, he isn't as free with me around. He has a sense that he's not alone, and he's always on guard, protecting his freedom."

"It'll come with time," Ben reassured her.

"I hope so. I'll head on down and wait for you there."

Amy made her way to the bottom paddock, and, as usual, Dazzle careened away at her approach. She climbed onto the gate and quietly sat observing him. After she had been sitting there for a few minutes, the stallion relaxed enough to snatch a few mouthfuls of grass. But as Ben strode down the path, Dazzle stamped his hoof, threw up his head once more, and cantered to the far end of the paddock with a shrill whinny.

Ben leaned against the gate. "He's so wired," he observed. "How are you going to get close to him? It seems impossible, unless you're going to force it — and I know you won't do that."

Amy slipped down from the gate. "Monty Roberts used join-up techniques when he gentled mustangs," she said. "But he's, like, the world expert on join up. I think I just have to start by letting Dazzle get used to me."

She walked slowly into the field, but Dazzle kept his distance. As she followed him around, he seemed to get more and more agitated. Soon, he was cantering frantically around the perimeter, his head craning over the fence, looking for an escape route, just as he'd done when he arrived. Amy felt anguished. The last thing she wanted to do was cause the horse additional stress, so she retreated back to the gate. A challenge? Dazzle was certainly that, and more.

"No good," stated Ben sympathetically.

Amy shook her head and climbed over the gate again. Ben looked thoughtful. "You know, there must be other people who've done this," he said. "Other people in the area, I mean, or not too far away. It might be worth your while asking their advice. I know you're brilliant with horses, Amy, but this is kind of new territory, isn't it?"

Amy thought about it. Ben was right. It was always a good idea to benefit from other people's experience.

"I guess I could look on the Internet during my lunch period tomorrow," she said. "Or I could ask Lou to contact the BLM and see if they have any suggestions."

As they walked up to the yard together, Amy was deep in thought. Ben's advice was sound. She'd read about gentling mustangs out West, and it wasn't easy. It took a lot of patience, persistence, and determination. She wasn't going to forget that.

"I know what I'm going to do," she said firmly. "I

think it's a great idea to talk to someone who's been through this, and I'll definitely try that. But I'm going to try join up tomorrow night as well. It might take hours, but I'll give it as long as it takes."

Ben looked at her knowingly. "Good for you," he said. "You never give up, do you, Amy?"

Chapter Six

As Amy and Ben reached the yard, Lou was running out of the farmhouse.

"The phone just never stops!" she called across the yard, shaking her head in disbelief. "I've been trying to sweep the barn, but my cell phone has rung about five times, then the phone in the house rang."

"Who was it this time?" asked Amy.

"Nancy," said Lou. "Confirming the arrangements for Wednesday."

"What arrangements?" Amy was curious.

"Looks like she and Grandpa are going on a date," said Lou with a coquettish smile. "So at least it was good news." She turned back toward the tack room. "And Willow's owners called. I said she was ready to leave, so they're coming to pick her up tomorrow. That's OK, isn't it?"

"Fine," agreed Amy, feeling a little sad, nonetheless. "But I'll need to talk to them and figure out how they should proceed from here. She'll still need careful handling so that her confidence doesn't take any setbacks. I'd like to stay in touch with them, if they'll agree to it."

"Well, I can explain the situation. I'm sure they'll agree to that, no problem," said Lou. "I'll say that you'll be in touch. Oh — have you discussed the new procedure with Ben?"

"Not yet," admitted Amy reluctantly.

"What?" asked Ben, looking from Amy to Lou.

Amy felt embarrassed. She still hated the idea of getting everyone else to do the dirty work. "It's just that Lou was worried that I'm not spending enough time treating the horses," she said to Ben awkwardly. "She thought that if the two of you could cover the yard work, I could get more training done. You'll still be able to work with Blackjack and some of the others that are further along. It's just a case of freeing me up a little more."

Ben nodded thoughtfully. "That makes sense," he said reasonably. "I wish I could be more help with the treatments. I know I'm no replacement for Ty, but I'll do whatever I can."

Amy felt a pang of sadness as she looked at Ben's tired face. He had worked so hard since the accident. He was more committed than ever. But she couldn't deny that he was right — no one could replace Ty. They had been trying to continue with the horses and the workload as if nothing were different, but Amy knew nothing was the same, and she wondered if it ever would be again.

✥

Dusk was beginning to draw in, but Amy was determined to do some more work with the horses. She realized that tonight would be her last chance to spend time with Willow, and she decided to give her a thorough brushing and some T-touch as a going-away present. She grabbed a grooming kit and headed to the bay pony's stall.

As she approached, there was a friendly whicker from the adjoining stall, and a young, curious head poked out over the half door. It was Solly, the boisterous yearling that had been sent to Heartland to learn good stable manners.

"Hi there, Solly," Amy greeted him. She reached out and scratched his neck, glad to see how bright and calm his eyes were. He had been one of the horses to catch equine flu, and his case had become dangerous when it developed into pneumonia. Solly's condition had been dire, but he had pulled through, and as he recovered, he had naturally become more gentle and responsive to the people around him. While he was now easier to work with, Amy was pleased that he was still full of personality.

Amy moved on to Willow's stall and realized how much Solly would miss his friend. The yearling was so attached to her — the pair were pretty much inseparable. Amy knew she'd need to give Solly plenty of attention to help him get over his loss. She slid back the bolt as Willow nickered a greeting. "Hello, girl," she whispered. "You're going home tomorrow. I'm going to miss you."

She set to work sweeping the pony's neck and back, losing herself in the rhythmic movements. Then, after finishing the grooming, she began to work her fingers in little circles, moving gradually from Willow's withers up to the top of her neck. Amy had never encountered a horse or pony that didn't love this treatment. It helped them to relax. She wondered if she would ever be able to do T-touch on Dazzle.

The next day at school, Amy spent her lunch hour in the computer lab, trying to find other people in the area who had adopted mustangs. She knew it was a long shot — even if there were a few mustangs nearby, it didn't mean she would be able to find out about them online. She tried all sorts of search combinations — mustang Virginia, Bureau of Land Management Virginia, gentling mustangs — but nothing came up. Then, just as the afternoon bell sounded, she had a breakthrough. She keyed in wild horse Virginia, and up came a promising site: *Patchwork: A Wild Horse in Virginia*. The computer area began to fill up with students in the afternoon class, and Amy feverishly scanned the Web page. "Patchwork, a striking piebald mustang, came to Virginia eighteen months ago . . . after a long gentling process . . . ideal riding horse . . . thanks to patience and hard work . . . " Amy scrolled down to the bottom. "Ed and Dolores Winters," she read, followed by a Virginia telephone number. Quickly, she scribbled it down, threw her notebook into her bag, and dashed to her next class.

The afternoon dragged on. Amy often found herself drifting off, her mind on the horses at Heartland. Now that she had both the early mornings and the evenings for treatment, there was so much more she could do, and she sat planning it all out. She would do a session with Candy every day — it would make it easier to establish the pattern to her problem behavior.

She could do a short session with Silver almost every day, too. Silver was a gentle mare that had come to Heartland for retraining. Her original owner had been forced to stop riding due to a knee injury, but she had been reluctant to part with Silver because she was so fond of her. After four years, the owner was finally forced to sell the mare. But Silver had grown rusty after the long stint without regular work. Accepting a rider again had proved to be a big readjustment, so her new owners had brought her to Heartland. Thanks to the mare's willing nature and earlier training, Amy was making fast progress. Silver would be back to form in no time.

Dazzle posed the real challenge. Amy thought of her plan to try join up and grew impatient with excitement. Why wouldn't the day end?

"Amy! Please get back to your work," her teacher reprimanded.

Amy jumped and realized she'd been gazing out the window for about ten minutes. She bent over her books once more.

❧

It had started to rain when Amy left school, a cold, driving rain that had her shivering in her clothes as she rushed along the Heartland drive. Joining up with Dazzle wasn't going to be easy in weather like this. She went upstairs and changed into her warmest work clothes.

"I'm going to try join up with Dazzle," she told Lou, shrugging on her slicker in the kitchen. "It might take hours, so go ahead with dinner."

"Well, OK, if you say so. Is there anything I can do?"

Amy shook her head. "Not really. I just have to stick with it."

"Good luck," said Lou, with a smile. "Hope it goes well."

Amy smiled briefly and headed out. To her surprise, she found that she was now feeling slightly nervous. She wanted this to work. She *needed* this to work. If she could manage some sort of breakthrough with the mustang, it would take a lot of pressure off all the other work she had to do.

Dazzle was standing with his hindquarters to the wind and rain, his tail tucked between his back legs. Amy had an image of him out on the plains, standing in the same position against swirling gusts of desert dust. She took a deep breath and entered the paddock.

As usual, Dazzle raised his head in alarm and galloped away from her. Amy followed him, breaking into a jog. As he slowed down at the far end of the paddock, she caught up with him, sending him cantering along the fence. That was the idea — to keep him moving on, to not allow him any rest until he accepted the alternative, which was to stop and be with her.

Amy followed him around the perimeter of the fence. Dazzle broke into a sharp canter whenever she drew near, making it difficult for her to keep him on the go; he had so much energy, and she began to tire of jogging after a few laps of the paddock. Out of breath, she slowed to a walk and marched after him with determination. As she drew near him again, the stallion rolled his eyes and whirled away. He screamed his anger in a high-pitched whinny. But after forty minutes, there was no sign of any submission. Dazzle was used to much longer treks.

The wind blew a blast of rain into Amy's face, and she wiped a damp strand of hair out of her eyes. *Just keep going,* she said to herself. *This has to work. It always does in the end.* She settled into a rhythm, marching forward, catching up with the stallion just as he slowed down again, waving with her arms to catapult him into action once more. The dull gray day began to darken, but she didn't stop. She lost track of time, trailing him around the paddock, backtracking as the stallion weaved to one side, trudging forward as he trotted, head high, down the side of the fence.

Weariness began to overtake her. She forced herself to put one foot in front of the other mechanically, keeping her eyes fixed on the stallion's. His fury was undiminished as he snorted once more and tossed his head in defiance. Amy's will began to deteriorate. *He's stronger than I am,* a voice whispered in her head.

The light was fading fast, and the rain began to fall more heavily. Fighting off tears of exhaustion, Amy summoned all her energy for a final effort before the darkness overwhelmed her. She lunged forward. Then, as the stallion cavorted away from her once more, she heard a voice break through the pounding of the rain.

"Amy! Are you OK?"

It was Ben. Amy paused and realized that her legs were trembling with fatigue. Her shoulders sagged, and she made her way over to the gate.

"How's it going?" asked Ben.

Amy shook her head, disappointment bringing a lump to her throat. "No good," she managed to say.

"Hey, come on. You can't stay out here in this," said Ben. "You've been at it for three hours. You're going to get sick. Lou sent me down to say there's some hot soup waiting for you in the farmhouse. You look like you need it."

Disconsolate, Amy reached for the latch and let herself out of the paddock. She was beginning to shiver, and Ben put his arm around her as they walked to the yard.

"He's so wild and tough," she whispered. "I don't know how I'm going to reach him."

"You will," said Ben firmly. "This is only the start. You'll find a way, I'm sure of it."

❧

"What you need is a hot bath," said Lou, putting a steaming bowl of chicken soup in front of Amy. "Eat that while I start running the water."

"It's OK," began Amy.

"Lou's right," said Grandpa assertively. "Some good hot food and a nice soak in the tub. We don't want you catching the flu."

Amy sipped a spoonful of the soup and felt it burn a fiery path to her stomach. She hadn't realized how hungry she was. As she ate, she felt her strength beginning to return. Grandpa sat at the table with her.

"So join up didn't go so well," he commented.

Amy shook her head. "He's so strong," she said. "It's going to take time."

Grandpa studied her face. "Are you sure you can cope with all this, Amy?"

Amy felt fatigue sweep over her once again, but she looked at Grandpa determinedly. "I'm not giving up on him," she said. "It's early yet. And Ben gave me an idea. He suggested I find other people in the area who've gentled mustangs and see how they've managed it. I found someone today at school, on the Internet."

"Well, you know best, Amy," said Grandpa, sighing. "You know we all trust you. But it's a lot for you, coping with the horses on your own. Mind you, I don't know what we can do about it, really."

"There isn't anything," said Amy quietly. "We're all doing as much as we can. You and Ben and Lou are dealing with all the stable stuff now. We just have to keep on going, don't we?"

Grandpa smiled gently. "Your mother would have said the same thing," he said softly. "I'm proud of you."

"Your bath's ready, Amy," said Lou, coming back in from the bathroom. "I put some lavender oil in it. That should help you relax."

"Thanks, Lou," said Amy, looking up from the bowl with a soft smile. "You make me feel like one of my own patients."

▬

Lying in the tub, Amy thought through her attempted join up once again. She'd never, ever known it to fail before. There had always been the beginning of a breakthrough after an hour or so, often less. But that was with horses that had interacted with humans from an early age. She knew, deep down, that even Monty Roberts had taken longer with mustangs, but she still couldn't help feeling a sense of failure.

She sighed and pulled herself out of the water. There was no point in thinking like that. She had to keep trying. She threw on her pajamas and a robe, then went to find her schoolbag and the Winterses' number.

Amy hesitated as she picked up the phone. It was difficult enough calling someone out of the blue, but it was even worse when she felt that so much depended on her work with Dazzle. She listened anxiously as the phone began to ring.

A man's voice answered breezily. "Hi, Ed Winters here."

"Hello, Mr. Winters," said Amy. "I hope you don't mind me calling you. I found your number on your Web site. My name's Amy Fleming. I was wondering if I could talk to you about your work with mustangs."

Quickly, she told him about the work she did at Heartland and Dazzle's recent arrival. Ed Winters listened intently, asking questions every now and then.

"Well," he said when she'd finished, "Dolores and I would love to meet you. Why don't you come over here and see our horses for yourself?"

"Are you sure? I mean, would that be convenient?" asked Amy.

"Anytime, just come on over," Ed Winters assured her. "We'd be more than happy to show you all we can."

"That's great," said Amy. "The sooner the better, in my opinion. Could you hang on a second?"

She hurried down the stairs into the den, where Lou and Grandpa were watching TV. "Lou, could you take me over to this farm after we go to the hospital tomorrow?" she asked. "I've found someone who might be able to help with Dazzle. They're just on the other side of town."

"Sure." Lou smiled. "Sounds like a plan."

Amy returned to the phone and made the arrangements. "See you tomorrow, Mr. Winters," she finished.

"Look forward to it, Amy," Ed Winters replied.

Amy put the phone down, feeling relieved. Even if join up hadn't been a success, at least she was putting another plan in place. She knew it was the only way — she had to keep looking forward.

Chapter Seven

Amy's sleep was restless that night. In her dreams, she paced relentlessly after the mustang, who always remained just beyond her. Plodding after him, constantly reaching out, she grew more and more weary as the roan appeared and disappeared way ahead of her. Then something shifted and it wasn't Dazzle she was chasing, but Ty, drifting in and out of a mist, fading, reappearing, and just as impossible to reach.

At last the alarm went off, and Amy lay still for a moment, pulling herself out of the dream world. *It's OK,* she thought to herself. *You're going to see the Winterses' farm today. You will find a way.* Then she forced herself out of bed and pulled on her jeans and a thick sweater.

As she neared the barn, Amy heard Solly whinnying,

calling to her over his stall door. Now that Willow had left, the stall next to his was empty, and Solly was clearly missing his friend.

"Hey there, boy," said Amy soothingly, going over to stroke his muzzle. "I'll give you a lick of honeysuckle remedy later. That'll make you feel better."

Honeysuckle remedy was great for stopping horses from dwelling on the past, and Amy had started giving the yearling a regular dose as soon as Willow's owners had picked her up. Amy thought it was helping. Considering all he had been through lately, Solly was coping well.

Amy led the yearling out of his stall and down the path toward the pastures. She still did a lot of leading work with him, teaching him to respond to pressure on his halter and to walk or trot neatly alongside someone without balking or pulling. He was so much more obedient than when he had arrived. Now he was usually well behaved, unless something distracted him.

After jogging up and down the track with him a couple of times, Amy was overcome with exhaustion. She was spent after her session with Dazzle the night before. Despite her plans to visit the Winterses, she felt disillusioned. She took Solly back to his stall and leaned against the wall, regaining her breath. She looked at her watch. Seven o'clock. A long day lay ahead.

❧

"Hey, Amy. Are you OK?" asked Soraya with concern when Amy got onto the school bus. "You're so pale. You didn't stay up with a sick horse all night, did you?"

"Not exactly, but close," Amy admitted. "I tried join up with Dazzle last night. I was running around the paddock for hours."

Soraya shook her head. "I wish I could help more, but it's difficult right now — Mom is always nagging me about my homework. She thinks I'm neglecting it because of the play."

Amy smiled at her friend. "Don't worry. We'll be fine. How is the play?"

"Great," enthused Soraya just as Matt got on the bus. He came and sat next to them as usual, and he and Soraya both chattered happily to Amy about how they'd just been fitted for costumes. Soraya tried to suppress a laugh as Matt explained that his Romeo tights were too short. He had finally convinced the director that they'd have to have new ones made.

Amy rested her head against the windowpane of the bus just for an instant. Then, suddenly, Soraya was nudging her. "Wake up," she was saying. "Hey, Amy. We're at school."

Amy opened her eyes to see Matt and Soraya exchanging grins and pulling her arm. "Coming," she muttered and followed them off the bus, trying to shake off her grogginess.

Soraya and Matt, by contrast, seemed full of energy all day, laughing and joking together. Amy grinned gamely at them and tried to join in, but her energy level was at a low ebb. And in any case, she knew there was something else behind their excitement. She smiled to herself at how much they were enjoying their time together.

She wasn't the only one to notice how well they were getting along. At lunch, the three of them happened to sit at the same table as Ashley and her friends. Right away, Amy saw that Ashley was keeping a sharp eye on Matt. She was ignoring her friends' conversation, trying to catch what Soraya and Matt were saying instead.

Soraya reached for the ketchup bottle and, as she did so, her fork fell to the floor with a clatter. Ashley smirked, but Matt leaped to his feet.

"I'll get you another one," he said, and walked off to the silverware station.

Ashley caught Amy's eye. "Don't you think Matt's letting that Romeo chivalry act go a little too far?" she said derisively. "What's happened to his taste?"

Amy regarded her coldly. "Why don't you keep your witty observations to yourself, Ashley?" she retorted as Soraya turned bright red. "And face the truth while you're at it — you're just jealous."

Ashley's eyes flashed. Amy's words had hit their target. She flicked her hair back over her shoulder. "As if I'd be jealous of anyone at that end of the table," she snapped.

"Well, yeah. And if you're trying to keep it a secret, cut the eavesdropping," said Amy. "It's a dead giveaway."

"Amy," Soraya said in a low voice. "Leave it alone. I couldn't bear it if Matt . . . "

Ashley turned away as Matt came back with a clean fork. He gave it to Soraya and stared at their tense faces curiously. "What's going on?" he asked. "Did I miss something?"

"No," said Amy hastily, cutting up her pizza. "It's nothing. Pass the water, please, Soraya."

Soraya smiled at Amy gratefully, and the moment passed.

❧

After school, Amy went straight to the hospital. It was Wednesday, and she felt bad that she hadn't visited Ty since Sunday. Usually she visited almost every day, but since Dazzle's arrival, her time had been more difficult to manage. She hurried up to Ty's room feeling anxious. Her stomach tightened as she considered who else might be visiting him She dreaded the thought of seeing Kerry-Ann.

To her relief, Ty was alone. He lay as still and silent as ever. Amy bent over him and placed a gentle kiss on his cheek.

"I'm here, Ty," she whispered and drew up a chair at his side.

She began to tell him all the news — how Ben and Lou were making more time for her to work with the horses, how Dazzle had resisted join up but how she was going to visit another mustang later that evening. As she sat there recounting all her various attempts to connect with Dazzle, she had a sudden vision of the stallion in the rain, spirited and independent, craving his freedom.

"You know, Ty, he's unlike any horse I've worked with before. He's not angry or afraid. He's proud. When I watch him, I wish I could return him to the wild, where he belongs," she heard herself saying. "Gentling isn't right for him. He's too spirited. I'm not sure he'll ever be truly happy with humans. He should be free."

She stopped and took in what she'd just said. Did she really believe that? The bond between horses and humans was incredibly precious, and most of the work at Heartland was about making that contact, cherishing it, and nurturing it. Had she really stopped believing that Dazzle could have as happy a life with people as he had had in the wild?

"I wonder what you'd say, Ty," she mused. She thought about it. Ty was so levelheaded and wise. He might take a more practical approach. It was difficult to say, just as it was difficult for Amy to make all the training decisions on her own.

As she was thinking, Ty's arm suddenly made an involuntary move across the bed. Amy's heart pounded for a moment. The arm lay still again, and she sighed. She was gradually getting used to this. At first, she'd thought that kind of movement could mean that he was coming out of his coma. Now she knew better. She looked at his face, willing him to open his eyes, but she knew that even if he did, it might not mean anything, either.

She smiled as Clare, the physical therapist, came in. Amy recognized her from previous visits; she spent a lot of time with Ty. She worked his muscles to limit their deterioration, in the hope that it would speed his rehabilitation period.

"I'm just going to do some work on his legs," said Clare. "Then I'll be turning him on his side. Don't mind me. You chat away."

Amy took Ty's hand and watched Clare's efficient movements as she manipulated Ty's leg, pulling and pushing it to restore the circulation and stimulate the muscles. She was a small woman, but Amy could see that she had strong, muscular forearms as a result of her work. Amy looked down at Ty's forearm. It was noticeably thinner than when he'd been working all day at Heartland. She stroked it gently, then turned to Clare.

"If — if Ty came out of his coma now," she said hesitantly, "how long do you think it would take him to get in shape again?"

Clare slowed her work for a moment and looked at Amy. "I can't really answer that," she said gently. "Coma patients vary so much." She hesitated. "Many don't come around at all. You do know that, don't you?"

Amy nodded. "Yes," she said quietly. "But I have to believe Ty will."

"Of course," said Clare. She continued to work for a moment. Then she added, "It all depends what part of the brain was damaged at the time of the accident. Some people make a full recovery. Others might have to work really hard to get their physical functions back. Or, in some, there might be loss of a particular mental function."

"You mean, like memory?" Amy asked nervously. "He might not remember people . . . or other things?"

Clare looked at her steadily. "It's impossible to know," she said frankly. "Like I said, I really can't predict one way or the other. I know it's hard, but you have to take Ty's condition one day at a time, as you've been doing. It's the only way, it really is."

Amy nodded, trying to suppress the panic that was rising inside her. If Ty couldn't walk or was very weak, she would know how to deal with that — she was sure she would — as long as she could talk to him and hear his ideas. But she wasn't sure she could bear it if he didn't remember her and the horses and all the work they'd done together at Heartland. That would be the worst thing imaginable.

Clare must have been able to see the horror on Amy's face. "Hey. You're letting your worries run away with you," Clare warned. "You don't know anything yet. One day at a time, remember?"

Amy let out a long breath and nodded. "Thanks, Clare." She stood up. "I'd better be going."

Clare smiled. "Sure. We'll take good care of Ty."

Amy walked down to the hospital lobby in a daze. She was surrounded by uncertainty. She felt like she couldn't count on anything — she had no guarantee that things would be even close to the same ever again. But Clare was right. She had to keep taking everything one day at a time. She tried to focus. She looked around the parking lot, scanning for Lou's car. At first she didn't see it. Instead, a figure hurrying toward the hospital doorway caught her eye. The person waved cheerily at the car that had dropped her off. Amy's mouth went dry. She knew that figure. It was Kerry-Ann.

Amy watched as Kerry-Ann disappeared into the building. Part of her wanted to run after the other girl and pull her back. *Why do you come here?* Amy wanted to ask.

Why does she come here, and what does she say? The thoughts flew through Amy's mind. *What if he can somehow hear her? What if she is there when he wakes up, and he remembers her? What if he remembers her, but not me?*

At that moment, the sound of a car horn frightened Amy from her thoughts. She looked out at the end of the sidewalk and saw Lou's car. Amy rushed forward and jumped in.

"How is he?" asked Lou. "No change?"

Amy shook her head silently. There was no point in saying any more. She fastened her seat belt, struggling with her feelings. Suddenly, she found herself in tears. She curled forward, the sobs convulsing out of her.

"Amy! Amy? What is it?" begged Lou. She put the car in park and leaned over to her sister, rubbing her back.

Amy buried her face in her hands, trying to stem the tears. "I just saw Kerry-Ann going into the hospital," she managed to say.

"Who's Kerry-Ann?" Lou inquired, trying to follow Amy's thoughts. "What on earth are you talking about?"

"Ty used to date her," Amy explained. "I heard Ty's dad talking about her. She keeps coming to see him. She gave him flowers last week, and now she's back again."

"Amy," Lou said, trying to calm her sister, "she's just an old friend. It's no reason to get upset."

Amy gulped some air, taking in Lou's words. "But why didn't he tell me about her?"

"I'm sure he wasn't keeping it from you. He just never had reason to bring her up. I mean, you've never had any reason to doubt Ty, have you?"

Amy looked at her sister and shook her head.

"Then you can't start doing it now. Amy, Ty loves you. I'm sure of that. And no matter what he might have felt for this other girl at some point, you are the only one now. You have to remember that."

"But what if she's the one he remembers — and not me?" Amy asked quietly, looking down at her hands.

"How could Ty possibly not remember you?" Lou rationalized.

"That's just what they said. He might not," insisted Amy.

"Who said that?"

"The doctors." Amy felt the ache of tears return. She couldn't look at Lou. She shielded her face with her hands, trying to gain perspective. But nothing was coming into focus. Everything was off. "Ty might not remember me," she blurted. "He might not remember anything. Not me, not Heartland or the horses, not . . . *anything*. That's what they just said."

"The doctors just told you that? But you said there was no change," Lou pointed out. "So there's nothing specific. They haven't found out anything new, have they?"

Amy recovered herself slightly. "No," she admitted.

"Nothing's changed. But that's part of the problem. I have nothing to go on. I don't know what to prepare myself for. I just know that I can't convince myself that everything will be okay if there is a chance that Ty won't remember me or Heartland. I just don't know how to deal with that."

Lou gave Amy's arm a comforting squeeze. "It's fine to fear the worst sometimes, Amy," she said. "We all do. But you also have to hope for the best. Ty's always been a fighter. We've got every reason to believe he'll pull through."

Amy sat still, studying her hands, and took a few deep breaths. Then she nodded and smiled at her sister. "You're right. Thanks, Lou."

Lou brushed a tear from Amy's cheek and started the car engine. "Now, where's this mustang farm? We should get going before it gets dark."

❧

They drove out of the hospital parking lot and turned in the opposite direction from Heartland. The Winterses' farm was located close to the main highway, and within twenty minutes Lou was turning into a leafy driveway. They passed a paddock on their right, and Amy caught a glimpse of three horses grazing. Seeing them, Amy was able to direct her thoughts to Heartland again.

"Hold on a minute, Lou," said Amy. "I think that's the mustang."

Lou slowed the car, and they peered through the trees at the horses. One of them was the striking piebald that had been pictured on the Web site. Amy recognized him immediately. She felt her anxiety lifting as she watched him. He was a beautiful horse, strong and graceful.

"He's the one in the middle, Lou," she exclaimed, pointing him out. "His name's Patchwork."

The mustang was grazing peacefully, swishing his tail. He heard the car and raised his head to listen for a moment before shaking his mane and reaching down to graze once again.

"He's lovely," whispered Amy. She thought of Dazzle's tense, frantic movements, comparing them to Patchwork's calm, relaxed amble as he wandered over to a patch of greener grass. "They've done a great job with him, you can see that."

Lou continued to the end of the drive. There was a neat block of stalls and a small farmhouse painted blue and white. It was pretty and well maintained.

"This place has a good feel to it," commented Amy as she and Lou got out of the car.

"Hi there!" called a voice. A slight woman in her fifties appeared around the corner of one of the small barns, pushing a wheelbarrow. She was no taller than Amy, but she was tanned and healthy-looking, with an overwhelmingly generous smile. "I'm Dolores," she said, putting down the barrow and extending her hand. "One of you must be Amy."

"That's me," said Amy, stepping forward and shaking Dolores's hand. "And this is my sister, Lou."

Dolores smiled and shook Lou's hand, too.

"We saw Patchwork on our way up the driveway," said Amy. "That was him, wasn't it?"

"That's right," said Dolores. "He's in with the other two. Helps calm them down."

"The other two?" asked Amy curiously.

"We've taken on two more mustangs," explained Dolores. "Things went well with Patch, so we thought, why not? Another gelding and a mare, both from the plains in Utah. We've only had them six weeks. I haven't had a minute to add them to the Web site. Ed tells me that's where you read about us."

Amy nodded, feeling more and more positive. If this couple had taken on three mustangs and were doing well with them, maybe there was hope for Dazzle after all.

"I'll just call Ed," said Dolores. "We'll head on down to see Patch before night sets in."

Ed posed a comic contrast to his wife. He towered above her in height and was almost as wide as she was tall, his cheeks rough and thread-veined. But he was just as cheerful and breezy as he had sounded on the phone. "Patch will enjoy this," he said, rubbing his hands. "He's a real show-off these days. Loves attention."

He led the way down to the paddock, striding ahead. As they neared the gate, they heard a bright whinny, and Patchwork trotted over, head and tail held high. Amy felt a thrill of excitement. The mustang clearly loved his new owners and was completely at ease in his new environment.

"How long have you had him?" Lou asked Dolores.

"Oh, it's eighteen months now," Dolores replied. "Though it feels like we've had him forever. Can't remember what life was like without him. You, Ed?"

"Nope," Ed responded. The piebald mustang was now by the gate, and Ed was scratching his neck. "Got any pony nuts there, Dolores?" he asked his wife.

Dolores fished in her pocket and brought out a handful. She offered them to the horse, who eagerly lipped them from her palm.

"He's so calm," said Amy in astonishment. "So . . . *tame*." It seemed an odd word to use, but somehow it was the only one to describe the difference between this gentle, affectionate creature and the wild stallion roaming the Heartland paddock.

Dolores laughed. "You should have seen him when he arrived," she said. "Tame was not the word. He was like some crazy beast."

"Well, if he was anything like Dazzle, you've done an amazing job," said Amy appreciatively. Then a thought occurred to her. "He's not a stallion, though, is he?"

"He was when he arrived," Ed told her. "We didn't have him gelded until the assessment year was up and he was ours for sure. The one you're working with is a stallion, that right?"

"Yes," agreed Amy as Ed unlatched the gate and they all filed into the paddock. They began to walk toward the other two mustangs. The mare was a golden dun color with a faint dorsal stripe, and the gelding was gray. The horses watched warily as the group approached, then moved off as they got closer.

"These two still like their own space," explained Ed. "We're taking it easier with them because it's our second go. Bit like having kids — you put all the worry into the first one."

"So what techniques do you use?" asked Amy. "Have you tried join up?"

"We did with Patchwork," said Ed. "We heard about Monty Roberts and read all his stuff, then put it into action. It wasn't easy, but it worked eventually. With these two, we've decided to give them a couple of months to settle in first. Being with Patch is good for them, and they get to see us every day. Nothing works like patience, that's what we've learned. We just come down here and say hi to them. They're getting used to it."

Amy didn't know whether to feel encouraged or dis-
couraged. Clearly everything was possible, in time —
but time was the one thing that was in short supply.
Dazzle was already taking her from other work, and she
hadn't made any progress. "So how long did join up take
with Patch?" she asked Dolores.

"Well, I tried a couple of times," said Dolores. "Trailed
him for hours but didn't get anywhere. Then Ed took
over and things started happening. Patch had all those
stallion instincts, you know? He was probably leading
his own herd before coming to us, so he'd been used to
protecting the mares. That can make it harder for a
woman to get a breakthrough. Stallions know the difference. They're used to rounding up mares, and they don't
take kindly to a woman trailing them."

Ed nodded in agreement. "It's a strange thing," he
said. "We used to train ponies for kids, and Dolores was
always the one to join up with them first. But not with
Patch."

"Don't let that put you off, though," said Dolores,
smiling warmly at Amy. "You just have to persevere.
Don't let him think he has one on you. That's my advice.
They're tough, these mustangs. They have to be. So you
need to be as tough as they are, up here." She tapped her
temple.

Amy listened, turning to Patchwork as she did so and
scratching his neck. The horse had followed them across

the paddock like a friendly dog, enjoying everyone's company and nudging pockets hopefully for more treats. She was thinking hard and trying to push away the obvious thought — *if only Ty could work with Dazzle.* She tried to hear the words of encouragement instead. Ed and Dolores weren't saying she had an impossible task on her hands. They were just pointing out the factors that were making it more difficult.

"I worked with him more once we'd achieved join up," Dolores continued. "Once we'd had the breakthrough, we decided he'd have to learn to work with me. So I stuck at it and it was worth it. We're the best of friends now. Aren't we, boy?"

Dolores joined Amy in rubbing the piebald's neck, and he gave a snort of satisfaction. Amy smiled. Patchwork loved the attention, all right. But somehow she couldn't imagine Dazzle ever behaving in the same way. Every horse was different, after all, and Amy just couldn't shake that sneaking suspicion that Dazzle was different, that he was too spirited to be tamed, that he was destined to remain wild forever.

The light was beginning to fade, and they all walked slowly back to the stable yard.

"It's good of you to visit," said Ed. "It's a pity there aren't more people who care about the wild horses. Truth is, we'd leave them out there where they belong if it were up to us."

Amy's heart warmed at these words. That was exactly the conclusion she'd come to about Dazzle's independent spirit. He should never have been taken from his herd. He might not really adjust to a tame, domesticated life. But at least there were some people who cared enough to train wild horses properly when they were forced away from their natural environment.

"I know what you mean," she said. She sighed. "It would be fantastic to see them running free."

"You've never seen that?" asked Ed.

Amy shook her head. "Only on TV."

"It's something else," Ed told her. "You should go out West sometime and see them — before it's too late and they're all gone."

"I'd love to," said Amy wistfully. "I'm sure it would help me understand Dazzle better, too. It seems worlds away."

❧

Ed and Dolores took them inside and showed them a home video. It showed Ed joining up with Patchwork, and Amy watched it intently. Just as she had done with Dazzle, Ed followed the mustang around the paddock, forcing him to keep moving when really he would have preferred to rest. It struck Amy, as she watched, how big Ed seemed in relation to the horse. It was easy for him to seem powerful and in control. She remembered how cold, wet, and huddled she had been when trying to join up with Dazzle and realized she must have seemed very small and insignificant.

She watched as Patchwork tired and began to give Ed the signals that he wanted to stop running, that he wanted to be with him. The first sign was a subtle movement of his ear, flicking it toward Ed as a way of showing his responsiveness. Then, gradually, Patchwork lowered his neck and made chewing motions with his lips. This was the horse's way of accepting his place in a herd's pecking order — they were signs of willing submission. It felt much, much safer for a horse to submit and be friends than to be alone, on the run.

Amy smiled as Ed stopped and slowly turned his back on the mustang. It was like a miracle. Now that the horse had accepted his position, he craved Ed's affection. He walked up to him of his own accord and nuzzled him on the shoulder.

Dolores shook her head as the recording came to an end. "That always kills me, however many times I see it," she commented. "It's just incredible."

"It is," Amy said. "That was amazing. Thanks for showing us. I hope Dazzle will get there in the end." As she said it, she tried to make herself believe it could happen.

"Sure he will," said Ed jovially. "Now, can we get you something to eat?"

Amy and Lou exchanged glances, but they knew it wasn't possible. There was too much to do at home. "That's really kind of you," said Amy. "But we really can't. We have to get back to Heartland. Thanks so much, anyway."

✦

Amy and Lou said their good-byes, then climbed back into the car. "It's been really helpful," said Amy, rolling down her window. "Would it be OK to call you if anything comes up with Dazzle?"

"Sure," smiled Dolores. "We'd be glad to help. Good luck."

Lou looked at Amy questioningly as they drove back down the driveway. "Was that really what you wanted to hear?" she asked quietly when they were out on the highway. "The stuff about men having it easier with stallions, I mean."

Amy frowned and thought for a minute. The issue about men and stallions wasn't what worried her, deep down. In a sense, it was positive in that there was an obvious solution — and an explanation for the slow progress. She was more worried that it might not matter who worked with Dazzle. It might be that no one could make him respond.

But if that was true, what would the future hold for him? He couldn't go back. It simply wasn't an option.

Even if Amy could convince the Abrahamses that he was an exception, that he was better off in the desert, there was no way the BLM would return him. His herd had been claimed by another stallion. And that meant that Amy couldn't go back, either. She had to fight and fight until she reached him. "There are never any easy answers, are there?" she said eventually. "But they didn't say I wouldn't be able to get through to him. They said it would take time. I can't give up, that's all."

"You know, there's always Ben," suggested Lou cautiously. "He might be able to help."

Amy considered it, then nodded. "Well, it might be worth asking him."

They drove in silence for a few miles. Amy felt weariness sweep over her and was just dozing off when Lou spoke again. She woke with a jump.

"It'll just be you and me and Scott at home tonight," Lou said. "I asked Scott to pick up some Chinese take-out. He should be there when we get back."

Amy was going to ask about Grandpa, but then she remembered tonight was his date with Nancy. "OK, sounds good. I hope he got some General Tso's chicken."

"I made sure it was on the order," said Lou, turning into the Heartland driveway.

"I'm just going to check on the horses," said Amy. "See you inside."

She headed off around the front stable yard and found

Ben in the feed room. He was finishing the last of the evening feeds.

"How's it going?" Amy asked him.

"Fine," said Ben, opening up a new feed sack. "Though I'm having a few problems with Red. He's kind of restless. I did a training session with him today, and he was all over the place."

"Really? That's not so good," said Amy sympathetically. "You're planning to hit the circuit again soon, aren't you?"

"Yeah. But . . . " Ben looked embarrassed, and he cut himself off.

"What?" asked Amy curiously.

Ben sighed. "The truth is, I'm not really spending enough time with him," he admitted. "There's just so much to do with Ty not being around. I know it's not anyone's fault, and I'm not complaining, but I can't see Red getting back in shape for a few months. Not at this rate."

Amy could tell that Ben was trying to sound practical and down-to-earth, but the disappointment in his voice seeped through nevertheless. "I'm sorry, Ben," she said.

"You don't need to be," he replied. "We're all in this together. We just have to prioritize, that's all."

Amy was touched. She knew that, deep down, Red and the world of competing were the things that kept Ben alive — they were his passion. If he was prepared to see them as secondary, it proved his loyalty to Heartland went deep. At the same time, it made her realize that she shouldn't ask him to take on any more. She thought of Lou's suggestion about Ben and Dazzle and decided to let it go. She would deal with Dazzle on her own — somehow.

❧

Amy did a round of the horses and checked that they were all comfortable. It was now dark and too late to do any work with them. Amy sighed with frustration. School, a trip to the hospital, and a trip to see Patchwork, and the day was gone.

The last horse she checked was Blackjack. He nickered a welcome, and she let herself into his stall. "Have I been neglecting you, boy?" she whispered to him. "I'm sorry."

She put her arms around his neck and hugged him, then gave him a quick scratch behind the ears. Before she knew it, she had instinctively begun T-touch, massaging Blackjack's neck in circular motions.

Ben's voice interrupted her. "I'm off now, Amy," he said over the stall door. "And I think Lou's wondering where you are. It's late."

"OK, thanks," said Amy. "See you tomorrow. I'll just finish up."

She gave Blackjack's neck a final pat, then headed to

the farmhouse. She'd forgotten all about the Chinese food. She found that Lou and Scott had left some out for her and were curled up together on the sofa in front of the TV. Amy spooned herself a plateful of food and sat down at the kitchen table on her own.

It had been a long day. Just like yesterday — and the day before. Amy felt as though she was battling against impossible odds. And while, as Ben had said, they were all in it together, there was no one else who really understood the work she was doing — no one to strive for the same goals with the horses, to celebrate each small success.

Amy heard Lou and Scott laughing in the other room and suddenly felt very alone. Grandpa was out with Nancy, Lou and Scott were happy together, and Soraya and Matt were growing closer day by day. But the one person Amy could really talk to, the person who understood everything she did, was lying in the hospital. Amy felt tears pricking behind her eyes and, angrily, she blinked them back. *Stop it, you've already been through this today*, she told herself fiercely. *There's no point in crying again. It won't change anything.*

But all the same, she wished she knew what would.

Chapter Eight

The alarm echoed through Amy's deep, dreamless sleep, pulling her reluctantly to the surface. Her whole body felt heavy. She didn't want to wake up — it was too soon — but the alarm insisted. Amy groaned and turned it off. It was six A.M. Time to start work all over again.

Groggily, Amy clambered out of bed and groped in the semidarkness for her clothes. She dragged them on and headed downstairs sleepily. Outside, the air was damp and chill, and it woke her up fast, like a slap across the face. She shivered and stamped her feet for a moment while she decided on the best way to make use of the two hours before school.

First of all, she wanted to see Dazzle. She walked down to his paddock briskly, thinking through what she had seen the previous evening at the Winterses' farm. She remembered again how big Ed Winters was and how he seemed to dominate Patchwork during join up. He was much more powerful in relation to Patchwork than she could ever be in relation to Dazzle. She was a great deal smaller, but there wasn't a lot she could do about that.

Then she had an idea. She couldn't make herself any bigger, but she *could* make it more difficult for Dazzle to keep his distance. She could work with him in a smaller paddock, or even one of the training rings. In a more confined space, she would be able to keep the pressure on him much more effectively and force him to acknowledge her presence. He would have to start interacting with her sooner or later. Amy clapped her hands in the cold air, feeling a rush of new determination. She might be on her own, but she wasn't going to give up. No way.

As she reached the paddock, she realized that moving the stallion would be easier said than done. No one had actually touched him since his arrival at Heartland — not since the battle to get him to the paddock. Amy thought of the Winterses again and how they were letting the new mustangs slowly get used to their presence. In spite of everything, Dazzle might be more accustomed to her now, too. Amy wondered if it was worth trying to catch him.

You're crazy to try, a voice whispered in her head. But

she didn't have much of a choice, did she? Amy opened the paddock gate.

As she approached, Dazzle raised his head and stared at her. Amy stepped forward a pace or two, then stopped. Dazzle didn't move. *He's not afraid of me*, thought Amy with satisfaction. *He knows who I am*. But that didn't mean he'd let her get any closer.

She decided to drive him slowly, carefully urging him into the far corner of the paddock. If she was really lucky, she might be able to catch hold of his halter as he tried to dodge past her. She reminded herself to keep her body language slow and quiet, and stepped forward again.

Dazzle shifted away from her, keeping his head low enough to snatch a mouthful or two of grass as he went. Amy knew that all his senses were alert to her, and she took her time, not wanting to alarm him. Slowly, they moved toward the corner of the paddock, with Amy pressing the stallion forward. *It's working*, she thought anxiously as they closed in on the fences to the front and to one side.

Then Dazzle threw up his head and stared at the fences. Amy held her breath. Now, as he turned to make his escape, she would get her chance.

Dazzle snorted, his nostrils trembling in the misty morning air. All at once he lunged into motion, whirling around on his haunches. In a split second, Amy was reaching for his halter as he thundered past. Her fingers made contact and she held fast, pulling the stallion back with all her strength. Amy felt her arm start to stretch against the stallion's momentum. Then the rest of her body was ripped from the ground, flailing next to the pounding of hooves, the convulsing muscles. But the motion stopped. Shocked to be fettered, to be held back, Dazzle skidded to a halt. Whiplash yanked Amy's arm. She scrambled to find her feet beneath her and looked up to where her hand still held tight. Dazzle's fiery eyes met hers. Then, with a scream of fury, he pitched his body forward and started to rear.

Amy was still grasping the halter, and Dazzle yanked her arm as he surged into the air. She couldn't let go. Amy wasn't sure what happened next. Everything seemed very still and calm. She felt something steadily loosen the grip of her fingers, gently uncurl her clenched fist — and suddenly, she was falling. She hit the ground, the blurred vision of the stallion's hooves high above her. The impact of the fall stunned her into action. She clambered out from beneath the mustang as his hooves thudded down. She looked at her hand, swollen and inflamed, and she realized she could not have let go on her own. Dazzle was too fast, and she had been in shock. It was as if something — or someone — had helped her release her hand. And she knew that someone was Ty.

She could feel his calming presence still. She traced

the leather burns on her hand. A visceral whinny broke through the air, and Amy looked up. Dazzle was cantering away to the other side of the paddock, and she was alone.

Amy sat up, feeling dazed. She looked around. There was no one in sight. The sensation of Ty's presence was gone.

She got to her feet and brushed herself off. She realized that her knees were shaking and that she'd just attempted something dangerous, something she should never have tried on her own. Lou and Grandpa trusted her when it came to the horses, and she'd let them down. She should have waited to approach Dazzle. She should have asked for help.

Amy walked over to the paddock gate and let herself out, casting one last look at the stallion. Dazzle was standing still, staring at her. Amy turned away and walked toward the barn with her head bowed. She felt shaken, partly because of the vision of Dazzle's hooves flailing over her head, partly because she knew she had allowed it to happen. She asked herself why. And deep down, she knew the answer. She'd been feeling alone and sorry for herself. She'd gone to the mustang's paddock believing there was no one to help her, that she was on her own to cope with everything. She had done something foolish, and she was lucky she had only a sore hand to show for it.

She reached the barn and picked up a broom. She wanted to do something practical to clear her mind. She started vigorously sweeping the yard.

"Hey, that's my job!" exclaimed Ben cheerily, coming out of the tack room.

Amy stopped sweeping and leaned on her broom. She gave a small smile. "You can have it back in a minute," she said.

"Amy, are you OK?" asked Ben uncertainly. "You're so pale."

Amy looked at him and sighed. "To be honest, I just had a close call with Dazzle. It was my fault; I should have called you. I just wanted to get him into the training ring so I could work with him there."

"On your own?" asked Ben incredulously.

"I know, I know," said Amy. "I thought I could manage. I didn't want it to be so complicated." She shrugged and started sweeping again.

"I wish I had known. I can help now, if you want me to," said Ben.

Amy thought about it. "Thanks, but I think he's too wired," she said. "He got all agitated when he realized I was trying to catch him."

The vision of Dazzle's hooves flashed before her again — and then the strange calmness that had followed. She hesitated, wondering whether she should mention it to Ben. Then she decided against it. It felt too private, almost sacred. She wanted to think about it on her own.

Sweeping the yard settled her mind. When she had finished, she decided to get Silver's tack. She could fit in a half-hour session with the mare before going to school. She knew it would help soothe her own feelings to work with a horse that had such a mild, accepting nature.

As she slid the bit into the mare's mouth, Silver nudged Amy affectionately with her soft nose. Her dark eyes were gentle and bright, her ears pricked forward. Amy smiled. She thought about the battle of wills that existed between her and Dazzle. He was such a contrast to the other horses at Heartland.

And then the memory flooded over her again, that feeling of Ty's presence, helping her, protecting her from the wild horse. *If he were here*, Amy thought, *Ty would know how to reach Dazzle.* Ty would have known how Dazzle would react to being manipulated and trapped. Amy was certain that Ty never would have tried to deceive him. But then again, if he were here, Amy never would have tried to capture Dazzle herself.

Amy pushed down the feelings of sadness welling up inside her and concentrated on the mare, sliding the saddle down over her withers and settling it on her back. Silver stood solidly as Amy reached underneath her for the end of the girth and then fastened the buckles. The horse followed willingly when Amy led her out of the stall.

Just as she lifted her foot to the stirrup, Amy heard someone calling her.

"Amy!" called Lou's voice. "Amy! Where are you?"

Amy looked around, her heart pounding at the urgency in her sister's voice. Instinctively, she felt that something important had happened. "I'm here!" she shouted. "What is it?"

Amy saw Lou running out of the farmhouse, pulling a jacket on, and her mouth went dry. Quickly, she led Silver toward her. Then, as Lou drew closer, Amy saw that her sister was smiling.

"Amy," she said in a rush, "Ty's mother called. There's been a change. Ty's started responding."

Amy stared at her, not sure how to react. "What? You mean he's coming out of the coma?"

Lou nodded. "It looks like it. She said it's still the early stages, and they don't know the full prognosis yet, but I promised to tell you right away."

Amy could hardly take it in. She flung her arms around Lou and they hugged each other, Silver's reins tangled around their shoulders. Unsure whether she was laughing or crying, Amy untangled them while Silver looked on, puzzled yet composed.

"I'll take you to the hospital now," said Lou, taking the car keys from her jacket pocket.

Ben had overheard the news and ran forward to take

Silver. "Leave her with me," he said to Amy, grinning. "Just go!"

Amy didn't need any encouragement. She and Lou ran to the car and set off.

"So what did Ty's mom say, exactly?" quizzed Amy as the car sped toward the hospital. "Do you know what happened?"

Lou shook her head. "Not really. There's been some sort of change in his responses, but she didn't say what. She sounded excited, though, so I guess it's pretty important."

Amy's mind was racing. "Do you think he said something?" she demanded. "Maybe he tried to sit up. What did she mean by a 'change in responses'?"

"I have no idea," said Lou. "Sorry." She gave her sister a grin. "Look, we're almost there."

Amy felt almost desperate with impatience. It felt unreal. Just moments ago, she had thought she felt his presence and now . . .

Questions burned through her mind. Would Ty recognize her? Would he still love her? Would he remember the accident?

Then she pushed them all away. He was getting better, that was the important thing. It was almost over. *Nothing remains difficult forever*, she thought. *Everything changes*. . . .

Lou dropped her off in front of the main doors of the

hospital. "I'll be up after I park the car," she called as Amy scrambled out and slammed the door.

Amy ran into the hospital and onto the elevator. When she reached Ty's floor, she was disappointed to find that everything seemed normal. For some reason, she had expected there to be people running around in great excitement. But the corridor was quiet. She hurried to Ty's room and peered around the door.

Ty's mother was sitting by his bedside. Amy stared at the familiar image, puzzled, her heart pounding once more. Then she looked at Ty, lying on the bed. What was going on? He looked exactly the same. Had there been some kind of mistake?

Mrs. Baldwin spotted Amy. She stood up and came toward her with a big smile. "Amy!" she exclaimed, giving her a hug. "You got my message."

"Yes . . . but . . . I thought you said Ty was waking up," Amy blurted, almost unable to contain her disappointment. "I thought there was a change."

"Yes, yes. They think he is," Mrs. Baldwin assured her. She took Amy's hand and led her to the bedside. "Look."

She picked up a newspaper from the bedside cabinet, rolled it up, and waved it over Ty's face so that the paper's shadow cut across the sunlight streaming in through the window. Ty's eyelids flickered, and he seemed to rock his head back and forth with the movement, ever so slightly. Then Mrs. Baldwin walked around to the other side of his bed.

"Ty!" she called. "Ty, it's Mom. I'm over here. Can you turn to me?"

And, to Amy's amazement, Ty turned his head slowly toward his mother.

Mrs. Baldwin smiled. "You see?" she said. "It's a breakthrough. He knows we're here."

Amy sat down, trying to take it all in. This wasn't what she'd expected, and yet Ty's mom was right. It *was* a breakthrough. But what exactly did it mean?

"What did the doctors say?" asked Amy anxiously. "Have they said he'll be OK? How long is it going to take?"

"Well, it'll take a while," said Mrs. Baldwin. "And it won't be easy. No one's saying that." She came and sat next to Amy by Ty's bedside. "But you know something? Deep down, I'd started to give up hope. And if you've lost your hope, you've lost everything. But that's all changed now. I know he's coming back to us." She reached over and squeezed Amy's hand.

Amy met her gaze and smiled. She felt a flutter of excitement in her chest. *Hope.* Mrs. Baldwin was right. She thought of the despair she'd been in only an hour or so before. Things felt very different now. She drew her chair closer to Ty's bed.

Just then, Lou rushed in. "Hi, Mrs. Baldwin. How is he?" she asked, hurrying over to the bed.

Amy explained what Ty's mom had told her. Then she leaned toward Ty.

"Ty," she called. "It's me, Amy. I'm here."

And just as Ty had turned his head toward his mother, he now turned it slowly — eyes still closed — so he was facing Amy.

Amy felt choked. Her eyes filled with tears. Lou put an arm around her shoulders and hugged her.

There was a noise in the corridor and the specialist came in with a small entourage of nurses and a medical student.

"Would you mind stepping outside just for a moment?" asked the doctor. "I'll be happy to answer your questions after I check on the patient."

Amy, Lou, and Ty's mom stepped out into the hallway.

"I'll get us all coffee," offered Lou. "Would you like some, Mrs. Baldwin?"

Ty's mom nodded gratefully. She and Amy sat down on the hard chairs in the waiting area. Amy felt like she was on tenterhooks. There were so many questions she wanted to ask.

"I wish Brad was here," said Ty's mom. "He's off on a trip. I called him on his cell phone. He's so happy that

Ty's coming back. This has changed him, you know. It's changed all of us."

Amy thought of Ty's father and all the problems that Ty used to have relating to him — how his father hated all the "horse nonsense." Amy looked at Mrs. Baldwin, feeling uneasy. Was everything really going to be that simple? "Yes. I guess it's changed me, too," Amy said quietly. She hesitated. "I worry, though, about how much it will have changed Ty — like, what he'll remember. And who. That kind of thing."

"Who he'll remember?" Mrs. Baldwin looked taken aback. She stared at Amy. "What do you mean?"

"Well," said Amy, desperately hunting for the right words, "they say he might not remember everything the way it was. He might only remember certain things. For example, he might not remember things that happened right before the accident. He might have forgotten things from the past several years, like the horses at Heartland or the remedies he used to know. But he might remember things from before, like Kerry-Ann." She stopped when she saw realization dawn on Mrs. Baldwin's face.

"Great heavens above, Amy!" exclaimed Mrs. Baldwin. "You're not worried about little Kerry-Ann, are you?"

Amy felt embarrassed. "Well, kind of," she admitted. "Ty used to date her, right?"

Mrs. Baldwin squeezed Amy's arm. "Honey, Kerry-Ann was our neighbor. She and Ty were sweethearts one summer, when Ty was just beginning to notice girls, but it didn't last. Then she moved away to the other side of town when he was about thirteen, and I think she's engaged now!"

Amy felt herself blushing. She hated sounding like a jealous girlfriend, especially when she knew, deep down, that her real worry was much more personal. She was afraid that Ty would have forgotten her. And even if he hadn't forgotten her, the accident could have changed him. He might not be interested in his work and life at Heartland anymore.

"Don't worry about a thing, honey," whispered Mrs. Baldwin. "Something amazing is happening. That's what matters, isn't it? Ty won't have forgotten you, I'm sure of it. You and Heartland mean far too much to him."

Amy swallowed the lump that was rising in her throat. Mrs. Baldwin was right. They had to concentrate on what was unfolding before them, the thing she had wanted so desperately all these weeks. She smiled and was trying to think of something to say when the specialist, Dr. Reubens, reappeared and invited them into his office. Lou arrived with the coffee, and they all followed the doctor down the hall.

"As you know, there's been a definite change," said Dr.

Reubens. "That's obviously a good thing. What we don't know yet is how full a recovery Ty can make — physically and mentally."

"When will you know?" asked Amy. "When will you be able to tell?"

"It all depends on how he reacts to stimulation," explained the doctor. "It's almost impossible to tell exactly how far someone's rehabilitation will go. The brain has to find its own way of compensating for the parts that have been damaged. Sometimes recovery is complete, but some patients never regain their full capacities. Once he's beyond a certain point, assuming he gets that far, Ty's own determination will play a big part. It's a long haul. He'll need to be a fighter."

Amy's heart swelled. She knew Ty wouldn't give in. He'd fight to get his life back. And she'd be there to help him every step of the way.

"Our task now is to offer as much stimulation as possible, both physical and mental," Dr. Reubens was saying. "The brain has to start kicking into life again. The initial signs are good, but please don't expect any miracles."

Despite the doctor's caution, Amy hugged herself with happiness. There was so much to hope for now.

Ty was coming back.

Chapter Nine

"Listen carefully, Ty," a nurse was saying. She was holding a carton of orange juice. She could squeeze its sides to make the juice rise into the straw. "I want you to nod if you'd like some more."

Amy watched intently. Ty was propped upright, his eyes closed. He didn't seem to be responding. The nurse was patient, but she was also willing to prompt Ty when necessary.

"I said, you need to nod if you want some more," she repeated. "You won't be getting any otherwise!" She turned to Amy and winked. "If he thinks he can have juice without asking for it, he's wrong. I won't let him. He can nod, and he knows it."

Amy smiled. The staff here were so strong and patient. They were pushing Ty further every day, demanding a response. Even as she watched, she knew that this nurse was working on two levels. She was asking Ty to think and decide what he wanted, and she was helping him regain one of the most essential functions of all, the ability to swallow food and drink safely.

It was a little more than a week since Ty's mom had first noticed a change. For Amy, it had passed in a blur. She had been astounded at the efforts made by the hospital team, by how many specialists were helping Ty regain his basic functions. He was now propped up for part of the day, during which he seemed to be awake, although he hadn't opened his eyes. He turned his head to follow sounds and movements as he had done on that first day; but now his movements were no longer involuntary. He was very weak, but if he moved, it was because he chose to.

"He nodded!" exclaimed Amy suddenly. "He did. I saw him."

"Did he?" said the nurse cheerfully. "Well, I'm sorry I missed it. He'll have to do it again, won't you, Ty?"

This time, Ty gave a definite nod. The nurse leaned forward and squeezed some more juice into his mouth. Slowly, with a gulp, he swallowed it. Amy drew her chair closer.

"Could you let me try?" she asked the nurse.

"Of course," the nurse responded. "How about you sit here or you'll spill juice everywhere. I'll need to stay with you, though."

"OK," said Amy. She traded places with the nurse and took the juice container. Then she turned to Ty. "Ty, it's me, Amy," she said in a clear voice. "Would you like some more juice?"

Ty remained still for a moment, and then, slowly, he bent his head forward in another nod. Amy grinned. It was inspiring to see Ty gradually returning to life. She leaned forward and gently squeezed more juice into his mouth. His rehabilitation hadn't been at all what she had expected. The progress was slow. Ty didn't offer any facial expressions. She had no idea what he was thinking, but Amy felt more secure with each passing day that he was improving. She found herself celebrating even the smallest improvements.

"He might have had enough now," said the nurse. "But he can shake his head if he doesn't want any more. We worked on that yesterday."

And that was just the case. The next time Amy asked, Ty managed to turn his head to one side. It wasn't exactly a shake, but the message was clear. Amy leaned back and handed the nurse the juice container.

"I should be going," she said regretfully. "But thanks for letting me help."

"That's what he needs," smiled the nurse. "Lots of help from the people he loves."

Amy turned back to Ty and put her hand on his arm. "See you later, Ty," she said softly. "I'll be back soon."

Amy wished Ty could see her smile when he rocked his head forward in a slight nod.

❧

Amy gathered up her coat and bag and headed down the hallway, feeling lighthearted. Things seemed to be going so much better now. It was difficult finding the time to visit Ty every day, but she was managing to fit everything in.

Every morning before school, she spent half an hour in Dazzle's paddock. She had decided against attempting join up again, at least for now. She thought it would be best to let him gradually get used to her, just as the Winterses were doing with their two new mustangs. She hoped he might be slowly accepting her. As she watched him each day, she tried to tell if his movements seemed less rigid, his eyes less fierce. She was hopeful, but she couldn't be sure.

"The Winterses called for you," Lou said when Amy got home from the hospital. "It was Ed. He said something about going to see a small herd of horses that belong to a friend. Sounded interesting. I said you'd call him back. How was Ty?"

Amy explained what had happened at the hospital. "He's starting to understand what people are saying to him," she recounted. "Then he nodded when I said I'd be back soon."

Lou gave Amy a hug. "That's good news!" she exclaimed. "I hope that's set your mind at ease."

"It certainly helps," agreed Amy, laughing.

She ran upstairs to change out of her school clothes, then came down and dialed the Winterses' number.

"Hey there, Amy," Ed said, his voice warm and welcoming. "Thanks for calling back. How's it going with that mustang of yours?"

"Slowly," Amy admitted. "But I think he's beginning to relax. I haven't seen the whites of his eyes in days."

"That's the way," said Ed. "Well, I've been thinking. An old friend of mine keeps a few horses out on his farm. He's got a lot of space, and he lets them run pretty wild. There's three or four mares and a stallion. He sells one of the foals every couple of years. I just thought maybe you'd like to go along and take a look. It's not the same as getting out West to see the mustangs, but I've learned a thing or two from watching his herd, all the same."

"That sounds amazing," said Amy. "I'd love to go. Where's your friend's farm, though? It's pretty busy here. I'm not sure how much time I can take off."

"It's about an hour from here," said Ed. "If we made an early start, you could see a lot in a morning and be back for a late lunch. How about it?"

Amy thought rapidly. It was Friday. Maybe, if she worked hard the next day, she could go on Sunday morning. She'd miss Grandpa's Sunday brunch, but she was sure he'd understand.

"How about Sunday?" she suggested.

"That'd be grand," agreed Ed Winters. "I know you're busy. I'll come and pick you up first thing. I'd love to take a look around Heartland, to be honest. Is seven-thirty OK with you?"

"That's great," said Amy. "I look forward to it."

Amy went out onto the yard. It was early evening and getting too late to do any training. Instead, she decided to visit Sundance, her loyal pony, who was in danger of feeling neglected. He was in a stall in the back barn. She found him pulling on his hay net. Amy unbolted the stall door and slipped inside. Sundance nickered a greeting, then continued chewing.

"Hello, boy," whispered Amy. "Have you missed me?"

She rubbed the pony's neck, then checked over his legs. He had recently recovered from a pulled tendon, which had taken a long time to heal, and he still wasn't totally fit. Amy straightened up, pleased to find that there was no heat around the tendon. "I wish I had time to ride you more," she told him.

There had been a time when Amy and Sundance had competed together at shows, before Storm had arrived.

Now she was really too big for him and, in any case, when she sold Storm, she had decided that her competing days were over. But Sundance was part of so many memories. Memories of sunny days on the trails, memories of her mother, memories of Ty.

"I wonder if Ty remembers you," she murmured to the pony, but she knew there was still no way to be sure.

Saturday was one of the busiest days that Amy could remember. She spent the usual amount of time with Dazzle, then worked with Solly, Candy, Blackjack, and Silver in quick succession. After lunch, a new horse arrived to take Willow's place, a beautiful chestnut show horse named Gold Dust. He had recently developed an intense fear of noises, shying at even the most common sounds. His owner said that he had been involved in an accident with a sheet of tarpaulin and that Gold Dust's anxiety had become increasingly disruptive to their training sessions. Amy showed the owners around, then turned out the chestnut in the quietest paddock, hoping he would settle in.

By late afternoon, Amy was glad to flop into the car next to Grandpa, who had offered to take her to see Ty.

"You look beat," commented Grandpa as Amy leaned back against the headrest. "I think it's good that you're heading out to that farm tomorrow. You deserve a break."

"Thanks, Grandpa," said Amy. "I just hope it's useful. I can't afford to waste my time just now."

"Don't worry about that," said Grandpa. "Go and enjoy yourself for once. You have a lot of responsibility for someone your age, especially with Ty in the hospital. It's not good, you know, never to have any fun."

Amy looked at him impishly. "I wonder why you're saying that?" she said teasingly. "It wouldn't be because you've been having more fun yourself recently, by any chance?"

Grandpa laughed. "Well, life's a funny old thing," he said. "Full of the unexpected." He paused, then added, "Nancy's coming for lunch tomorrow, as a matter of fact. She'll be at Heartland when you get back from the farm."

"That's great," said Amy. "You can wow her with one of your brunch specialties. What are you going to fix?"

"I haven't planned the menu yet, Amy," he said, stealing a look at his granddaughter.

"Well, it'll be good to meet her. I bet she's nice."

They arrived at the hospital and headed up to see Ty together. As it was Saturday afternoon, the hospital was busy, and Ty already had several guests. His mom was there with his dad, who was back from his trip. One of Ty's old school friends, Felix, had also dropped by. Amy and Jack Bartlett said hello and sat down.

"He's asleep," said Mrs. Baldwin. "I think we've worn him out."

Amy smiled. "Have there been any more changes today?" she asked.

Mrs. Baldwin nodded. "He's started making noises at the back of his throat. The doctors say he's trying to speak. They think he might manage it in a day or two."

"Really?" breathed Amy. "That's fantastic news."

"Isn't it?" agreed Mrs. Baldwin. "He's going to pull through, Amy. I'm sure of it."

Amy looked across at Ty's peaceful face, her heart swelling with joy. How she longed to really talk to him again and hear him reply.

Felix soon left, then Ty's mom said she needed to head home to get ready for work. The Baldwins stood up and said their good-byes, leaving Amy and Grandpa by Ty's bedside.

"We ought to be going, too," said Grandpa gently.

Amy nodded, reluctantly. "May I have another ten minutes?" she asked.

"Of course," said Grandpa. "I'll head down and wait for you in the car."

"Thanks, Grandpa," Amy replied.

When Jack Bartlett had gone, the room seemed very quiet. Amy listened to the sound of Ty's breathing and studied his face. It was good to be alone with him, even if it was just like this.

She reached for his hand and squeezed it in her own. As she did so, Ty stirred. Amy shook his hand slightly, hoping he might wake. His eyes fluttered open. Amy knew he'd done that before. Even in the depths of his coma, he had sometimes stared out at the world without seeing. But now he could focus and register the world around him.

"Ty?" she whispered.

His eyes traveled over her face, still looking hazy from sleep.

"It's Amy," she continued.

Amy watched as Ty's eyes began to focus more clearly. She looked into their depths, searching for clues to her constant question: *Do you remember me?*

Then a faint smile appeared on his face, and he opened his mouth. Amy held her breath.

"Are you okay? Can I get you something?" she asked.

A mumbling sound rose from Ty's pressed lips. "Mmmmm," he managed, then frowned and tried again, still looking at her face. "Ammmm . . . Ammmy," he said. "Amy."

"Ty!" Amy reached forward and hugged him, beside herself with joy. "You *do* remember me. Oh, thank you. Thank you so much."

❧

Even after Ty fell asleep, it was difficult for Amy to tear herself away from him, but Grandpa was waiting. She gave Ty's hand a final squeeze and left the room. Then she went to find the car, her heart bubbling. If Ty remembered her name, he must remember their relationship as well.

Back at Heartland she got back to work, feeling buoyant. She had fun working with Solly, who was in a skittish mood, butting her playfully with his head. Amy laughed happily at the yearling's antics, not wanting to scold him. She felt too full of hope. It was difficult not to be when something so exciting had happened. It was so new, but it carried the promise of something old and dear.

Later, on her final round of the horses, Amy went down to check on Dazzle. As she walked toward the paddocks, the sound of neighing and squealing reached her ears. She broke into a jog, wondering what was going on.

She stopped in amazement as she neared Dazzle's paddock. He was cantering frantically up and down the fence, calling and squealing. And a horse was answering. Amy looked in the direction of the response. It was Gold Dust, the new horse in the next paddock. *But Gold Dust is a gelding,* Amy thought to herself. *Why would Dazzle be squealing at a gelding?*

She leaned on the gate. "Dazzle!" she called softly.

The stallion stopped and stared at her. Then he whirled around and bucked before thundering down to the far end of the paddock with a high-pitched whinny.

Amy felt slightly awed and puzzled. Dazzle seemed more angry and frustrated than he had been in days. But a gelding didn't pose any threat.

✎

Amy was still troubled by Dazzle's behavior the next morning as she waited for Ed Winters to pick her up. She was concerned that it might be some sort of setback, and Amy didn't know how much longer the Abrahamses would let Dazzle stay at Heartland if he showed no sign of improvement.

Ed Winters arrived promptly, and Amy quickly showed him around the yard, then took him to the paddock to see Dazzle.

"He's a fine-looking stallion," commented Ed. "I can see he's a handful for you, though. He's got fire in his eyes."

"Yes," agreed Amy, as they walked back toward his truck. "I'm not sure if I'm getting anywhere with him."

"You'd be surprised," said Ed. "You stick with it."

They climbed into his truck and chugged off into the morning sunlight. It was a lovely drive through some glorious Virginia countryside, with the autumn trees in spectacular hues of orange and gold. As they swept along, Amy began to enjoy herself. Grandpa had been right. She needed this.

The road led to true country, where the farms were set

farther apart, between the hills. Amy wound down her window to breath in the crisp air.

"This is Pete's place," said Ed, turning up a tree-lined driveway. The engine revved as they began to climb slightly, the gravel path winding up the side of a hill.

As they came to a slight clearing, Amy got the impression of a somewhat ramshackle setup — wide meadows that had neither been grazed nor cut, the parched remains of the long summer grass growing as tall as the fencing. There were other meadows that had returned to scrub and woodland, no upkeep to the fencing at all. Yet as she smelled the rich autumn aroma, she was filled with excitement. There was a wildness to the place that was exhilarating.

"Pete owns half the hillside," Ed explained as they turned yet another bend in the track. "It's been in his family for years. They don't do much with it now. No crops or firewood."

At last, they came to a house. Outbuildings were scattered around it. Amy climbed out of the truck and stretched her legs. The air was still, with only the sound of a woodland bird calling. Then the screen door of the house opened, and a tall, lanky man came out. Amy thought he looked to be about Ed's age.

"Hey there, Ed," he said.

"Pete, this is Amy," said Ed. Pete held out his hand.

Amy shook it and smiled. Pete looked down and away, then took a mighty breath and dug his thumbs through his belt loops. There was something about Pete that Amy couldn't put her finger on, something different. She followed the two men into a big, cavernous kitchen that looked as though it hadn't seen much cleaning in recent months. Sunshine filtered in through the windows, high-lighting dust motes that hung in the air. A couple of old pans stood on the stove.

"Don't get many visitors," said Pete, looking slightly apologetic. "Can't offer you much, though I have some coffee brewing."

"We're fine, eh, Amy?" said Ed, winking at her. "We're a little pushed for time. Say we just head on out there?"

"Sure, sure," said Pete. "I'll just finish up."

He took a swig from a stained enamel mug, then led the way back outdoors. "We'll go in this," he said, indicating a muddy station wagon. "Gets a bit rutted out there."

They all climbed in, with Amy on the passenger side by the window. Ed handed her a pair of binoculars he had found on the floor. "These might come in handy," he said.

They set off on a track that led behind the house and up the hill. The trees quickly gave way to more open land, the same kind of unkempt grazing land that Amy had seen earlier, but slightly rougher.

"Any idea where they are?" Ed queried, looking at Pete.

"Last time I saw them they were out on the east side," said Pete. "We'll head that way first."

The track soon dwindled to nothing, and the car bumped over the rutted ground, making for slow going. Amy trained the binoculars over the land ahead, scanning the horizon for any sign of the horses.

Suddenly, out to her right, she saw them. "There they are!" she exclaimed.

Pete swung the vehicle around and headed in the direction of Amy's outstretched arm. Amy peered through the binoculars, trying to keep them focused as the car lurched to and fro. She could make out three horses close together and another two slightly to one side. She wasn't sure, but it was possible there was another horse hidden behind the group.

The horses heard the car approaching and raised their heads in alarm. Pete came to a halt. "They'll start moving now," he said. "Best to watch them from here."

With the car stopped, Amy could pick out the horses more clearly. It quickly became obvious which one was the stallion. He was a dark bay, more muscular than the mares, and at the sound of the car he began to round them up. Snaking his head down low, he chivied the mares together, then urged them away toward the brow of the hill. As he did so, Amy saw that the sixth horse was young — a yearling, no more.

"Will you be keeping that one, Pete?" asked Ed.

Pete shook his head. "Nope. He'll have to go. The stallion will drive him out regardless, and there's nowhere for him. Can't live on his own."

"Ah, he's a colt. Can't tell from here," said Ed.

The horses trotted away, and Pete started the engine again. As they slowly bumped their way after the mustangs, Amy thought about the way herds worked. She knew that a stallion remained in charge until he was challenged by a younger, stronger male, and that any young males were driven away to find herds of their own. That's what Pete meant when he said there was nowhere for the colt to go: There were no other horses on the hillside. But horses never remained solitary for long. There was safety in numbers, and young stallions often grouped together for company until they claimed mares of their own.

Then she remembered her experience the night before, seeing Dazzle squealing after Gold Dust. She suddenly understood. *Dazzle was lonely.* He had been alone in this paddock ever since he arrived. He was a stallion plucked straight from the wild, a stallion used to having a whole herd to interact with, to protect. Dazzle was interested in Gold Dust simply because he was another horse.

Amy turned to Ed. "I think Dazzle is missing his herd," she said. "He's lonely, I know he is. Did Patchwork go through that, too?"

Ed nodded. "Sure," he said. He nooded knowingly at Amy. "But that's the key. People can become part of the herd as well, you know."

Of course, thought Amy. That was it! She had been so preoccupied with Dazzle's wild, fiery nature that she had forgotten to think of him as a herd animal. Herd animals needed company. It was what made them feel safe. In the long run, they would do anything to find the safety of the group again — and that could even mean accepting humans into the group.

They followed the herd for another hour, watching the stallion guide his mares, keeping them together and driving them from behind. It was fascinating. Amy could have happily watched them all day. But the morning was wearing on, and when the herd crossed a stream, Ed suggested that they turn back.

"Thanks so much," said Amy when they were back at the house. "I learned a lot. I'm very grateful."

Pete gave a bashful smile and shook his head. "Pleasure," he said awkwardly. "Sorry I couldn't offer a better welcome. The farm's lost its woman's touch, I'm afraid."

There was something about his shy honesty that made Amy warm to him. "I've enjoyed every minute," she said genuinely.

Ed shook Pete's hand, then he and Amy climbed back into his truck.

"You had a good time, then," commented Ed. "Thought you would. Pete's a peculiar character, no doubt. He lost his wife several years back. Really threw him. He's never been the same since, to tell you the truth."

Amy remembered her first impression of Pete. So that's what it was. A man living alone up in the hills. *Loneliness makes us all act a little out of character,* she thought. She smiled to herself as they headed back down the winding track to the main road. *It's not just horses that need one another,* she concluded. *Humans are herd animals, too.*

Back at Heartland, lunch was just over, and Grandpa was making coffee while Lou served dessert.

"Come in, come in," Grandpa said jovially. Amy thought his cheeks were slightly more flushed than usual, and it didn't take long to figure out why. "This is Nancy," he announced, placing his hands on the back of her chair. "Nancy, this is my granddaughter Amy and . . . Ed Winters, isn't it?"

"That's right," said Ed, sitting down at the kitchen table easily.

Amy smiled at Nancy who, in spite of being so much older than Amy, appeared a little nervous. She was about fifty-five, Amy guessed, but strong and fit, with beautiful blue eyes that made her look much younger. Then Amy glanced at Grandpa and realized that he suddenly looked much younger, too. There was a lightness about him that she hadn't noticed before.

Grandpa quickly heated up some food for Ed and Amy — burgers with potatoes and mushrooms — and placed it in front of them with a flourish. "There you go. Hope you don't mind us getting on with the apple pie," he said. "So how was your trip?" He turned to Nancy. "Ed took Amy out east to see a herd of wild horses," he explained.

"It was amazing," said Amy, launching into a description of what they had observed. "It helped a lot," she finished, smiling at Ed.

"Jack's been telling me about your work," said Nancy. "I think it sounds fascinating. I'd love to get a personal tour, when you have time."

"Of course," said Amy with a smile.

She dug into her food, feeling slightly wistful. She was so happy for Grandpa. He had been on his own for years, and Nancy certainly seemed very nice. But Amy was beginning to learn about loneliness. She thought of

Ty mouthing her name and longed to have him back. And although she knew she would stick by him whatever happened, she also knew, deep down, that it was the Ty who cherished her and Heartland that she wanted most of all.

There was a knock at the door, and Soraya poked her head into the kitchen. "Hi, everyone!" she called gaily. "I'm not interrupting, am I?"

"Soraya! Come in," said Amy. "We're just finishing lunch."

Soraya stepped in, and Ben leaped up to find her a chair in the crowded kitchen.

"Oh, I don't need a seat, I've come to help," said Soraya. She was clearly in a good mood, chatty and cheerful. "I haven't been over for ages. What can I do?"

"Where d'you want to start?" laughed Amy.

"I was thinking of taking Red out on the trails," Ben piped up. "You could come with me on Silver."

Soraya frowned and hesitated. "I was thinking I might be more help around the yard," she said apologetically. "Sorry, Ben." She looked at Amy. "Unless that's what you want me to do?"

Amy saw the disappointment on Ben's face and sized up the situation quickly. Soraya had changed recently. She didn't leap at every opportunity to be with Ben the way she used to. And knowing what she did, there was no point in pushing it.

"Well, I really don't mind," she said carefully. "Any help would be great. But I could use an assistant when I work with Solly, if you're up for that. And a lot of the tack needs to be cleaned — no surprise there."

"Sounds fine," said Soraya. "I'll go out and start on the tack while you all finish up here. See you guys." And with that, she bounced out of the kitchen.

Ben concentrated on his coffee and avoided Amy's gaze. She felt a pang of sympathy for him, but there was nothing she could do. She stood up and cleared away her plate, along with Ed's.

"That was delicious," said Ed. "Thanks very much. I'd better be heading off. Dolores will be wondering what happened to me."

"No apple pie?" offered Lou.

Ed patted his stomach. "No, that'll do me fine, thanks," he said. "I'll be on my way."

"I'll see you out," said Amy, grabbing her coat.

They walked back to Ed's truck, and he climbed into the driver's seat.

"Thanks so much for your help, Mr. Winters," Amy said. "The trip gave me a lot to think about."

He smiled. "You're closer to a breakthrough than you think," he told her as the engine roared to life. "I'm sure of that."

Amy waved to him and went to find Soraya in the tack room. Her friend was just lifting down one of the saddles from its rack.

"Before you get started, d'you want to come and see Dazzle?" Amy asked.

"Love to," said Soraya. She put the saddle down and walked with Amy toward the paddocks, chatting away about her rehearsals. "You will come and see the show, won't you?" she begged.

"Of course I will!" Then she pointed. "There he is," she said, indicating the roan mustang that, for once, was grazing near the paddock gate.

"Wow! He's beautiful," exclaimed Soraya.

They stopped walking for a moment so as not to disturb him. But the mustang's ears, so finely tuned, had already picked up their approach. His head flew up, and he stared at them. Then, much to Amy's astonishment, he simply snorted and returned to cropping the grass.

"He usually races down to the other end of the paddock, wailing the whole way," Amy said to Soraya in a low voice. "Let's get closer."

They stepped forward softly toward the gate. Dazzle looked up again.

"Hi, Dazzle," said Amy gently, expecting the stallion to gallop off at the sound of her voice. But he didn't. Instead, he shook his mane and continued to graze. Then, from deep in his throat, came a nicker of welcome.

Chapter Ten

❧

"That's amazing!" exclaimed Amy, gripping her friend's arm. "He's never done that before."

She and Soraya leaned on the gate. Now that they were closer to him, Dazzle grew nervous and trotted a few steps. But he quickly returned to grazing once more, staying near the gate.

Amy watched him intently. "I learned something today," she told her friend. "Seeing the herd up in the hills reminded me that horses hate to be alone. I'm beginning to think that Dazzle might need my friendship."

"That would make sense," said Soraya thoughtfully. "It's sort of the same idea behind join up, isn't it?"

Amy nodded. It was true. "Yes. In join up, you make the horse feel alone by driving him around the ring. In the end, he chooses your friendship. But Dazzle's so proud that it's taking him more than a few hours to make up his mind."

"Everything takes time, doesn't it?" sighed Soraya.

Amy nodded. "Sure does."

They walked back up to the yard, and Soraya returned to the tack room. Amy decided to continue her work with Solly. She was teaching him to load into a trailer and unload again without fussing — he still had a tendency to get distracted and pull against the lead rope. But just as she was bringing the yearling from the back barn, she heard Lou's voice calling her.

"Amy! It's the phone!" Lou shouted. "It's Mrs. Baldwin. She wants to speak to you — now!"

Hastily, Amy returned Solly to his stall and ran to the house. "Did she say what she wants?" she asked as she opened the door to the kitchen. "Is it about Ty?"

"I don't know," said Lou. "I guess it must be."

Amy snatched up the phone breathlessly. "Mrs. Baldwin? It's Amy."

"Amy! Is there any way you could come to the hospital right away?"

"Of course!" exclaimed Amy. "I'll ask Lou to bring me over. I'll be there as soon as I can."

Amy's mind was racing as they drove to the hospital. What had happened? Had Ty made a sudden leap forward? Her imagination ran wild. Perhaps he had started to walk, or maybe he'd said something important.

"Don't jump to conclusions," said Lou, seeing Amy's excited expression. "Wait and see what's going on first."

"I'll try," said Amy with a grin, trying to calm herself down.

They reached the hospital, and Amy ran inside. She waved good-bye to Lou, rushed up to Ty's floor and found Ty's mom in the hallway outside, pacing up and down. Amy touched her on the arm.

"Oh! I'm so glad you're here," said Mrs. Baldwin.

"May I see Ty?" asked Amy.

"Of course."

Resisting the temptation to quiz her, Amy stepped into Ty's room. There, an astonishing sight met her eyes. Ty had made great progress physically. He was sitting in a wheelchair by the side of his bed. A nurse was trying to help him eat some lunch with a fork. Amy recognized her as the same nurse who had helped Ty learn to swallow again, with the orange juice. But this process was altogether different. As Amy watched, Ty's face contorted in anger. Clumsily, he reached for the fork in the nurse's hand. She gave it to him, curling his fingers around it. But almost immediately, he dropped it.

"No!" Ty managed to cry out. And with a sweep of his arm, he sent the lunch plate crashing to the floor after the fork.

Amy's mouth went dry. She stepped forward, with Mrs. Baldwin at her side.

"Ty," she exclaimed. "What's wrong?"

Ty turned toward them, furious. His mouth worked, trying to form words. At last he managed to get them out. "Go . . . way," he said. His voice was brittle and harsh.

The nurse, who was patiently clearing up the mess on the floor, looked up at Amy. "D'you want to wait outside for a minute?" she said. "I'll get the doctor to speak to you."

Amy took Mrs. Baldwin's arm. She understood why Ty's mother had called her so urgently. It wasn't what she'd imagined at all. This was horrible. She felt cold inside. What was happening to Ty?

They sat outside in the waiting area for a few moments. Soon Dr. Reubens appeared.

He smiled and sat down next to them. "Ty has made tremendous progress over the last few days. Still, I expect his behavior has come as a bit of a shock," he said.

"Ty's just not like that," said Mrs. Baldwin in a trembling voice. "He's not the same person. That's not my son. We haven't lost him, have we?"

"It's still too soon to tell exactly how far his recovery is going to go," said the doctor carefully. "So far, Ty is adapting to the new challenges well and exceptionally fast. But we are dealing with a lot of unknowns. What I can say is that his behavior is not unusual. It's normal for coma patients to be somewhat out of kilter. Their personalities can seem to have changed, but that's often not the case. Patients can feel off balance, and it can take them a long time to find the right balance again. Until they do, they might find their limitations frustrating."

Amy listened in silence, trying to take it all in.

"He told us to go away," said Mrs. Baldwin softly. "That was the hardest thing of all."

"You can't take Ty's behavior personally," said the doctor. "He is thinking and reacting and feeling. Those are all good things. He needs you, now especially. He needs you to be a constant for him. He needs to be able to rely on you. And he needs you to be patient."

"We can do that," said Amy bravely. "We'll stick with it. May we see him again?"

"Yes. Just keep in mind that he's struggling with his motor functions. That means the way he operates his limbs and holds things. It's frustrating for him when he can't do something. He probably feels like a child, learning everything from scratch. But you can help him by being there and being persistent. Just try to ignore the mood swings."

Amy and Mrs. Baldwin headed back to Ty's bedside, where the nurse was trying again with a fresh tray of food.

"He wants to hold the fork himself," explained the nurse. "But his fingers just won't grip hard enough yet. It's a real battle, isn't it, Ty?"

Ty stared at the fork in the nurse's hand and nodded. Then he reached for it again. Amy stepped forward, and as Ty's fingers touched the fork, she curled her own fingers around his, helping him to bend them inward. The nurse let go, and for a moment, Ty had the fork securely in his grasp.

A slow smile spread across his face, and Amy felt such pride. But then, as she withdrew her hand, his fingers loosened and the fork, dropped once more to the floor with a mocking clatter. Ty's face creased in frustration and he gave a howl of anger, banging his other arm against the wheelchair.

The nurse stepped forward and picked up the fork. "Try again," she said softly to Amy.

After a long while, with the nurse, Amy, and Mrs. Baldwin taking turns, Ty had eaten almost the whole meal and was ready to get back into bed. Mrs. Baldwin motioned to Amy.

"Can we talk?" she asked in a low voice. "You don't have to go home right away, do you?"

Amy shook her head.

"Let's go to the cafeteria downstairs," said Ty's mom. "My treat."

They sat in a booth along a wall of the hospital cafeteria. Amy got a milk shake and sipped it as Mrs. Baldwin blew on her coffee.

"I just wanted to thank you," said Mrs. Baldwin. "And I wanted to tell you something, too. Whatever happens with Ty, I'd just like you to know that I think you've been amazing during all this. I know how busy you are, with all those horses. I understand that it's not easy. But the way you've stuck by Ty — the way you care for him . . . " She trailed off, biting her bottom lip. "You've been great to me, too. You're very special, Amy," she finished.

Amy was unsure what to say. She smiled awkwardly. "Thanks, Mrs. Baldwin," she replied. She stared at her milk shake, stirring it with her straw. "I just hope he comes back. You know — *really* comes back. He was always so patient before, with the horses and everything. But I'll be here for him, whatever happens."

Mrs. Baldwin nodded and squeezed her hand. Amy looked up and met her gaze. She saw the same fear reflected back at her — her own fear, that things might never truly be the same. But she could also see hope and determination and love.

"I know what you mean," said Mrs. Baldwin. "He was the same as a child. Real patient and trusting. He'd sit for hours, trying to fix things that were broken or working on a tough puzzle. But even if he's never the same again, I'll still love him to the ends of the earth. Something tells me you will, too."

Amy felt a lump grow in her throat. She thought about what Ty had been like earlier, full of emotions she'd never seen in him before — the anger and violence and frustration that were so out of character. But she nodded. "Yes," she whispered. "I'll still love him, whatever happens. It's true."

Amy was relieved when the next few days passed quickly. She spent as much time as she could in the hospital each day after school, often seeing Mrs. Baldwin there. On one occasion, Mrs. Baldwin told her that Kerry-Ann's fiancé had found a job in Washington, D.C., and that she had left town to be with him. With all that had happened, the news sounded incidental. Amy thought of how thoughtful and generous Kerry-Ann had been, spending time with a friend she hadn't seen in years; Amy was almost disappointed that she hadn't gotten to know her.

Ty's father was a regular visitor, too, and seemed to be gradually accepting Amy's presence. He never said very much. Amy was simply aware that his greetings had slowly grown more warm and welcoming.

Being with Ty, though, wasn't easy. Amy had to steel herself for each visit. His moods were erratic. Sometimes he didn't respond at all to what was going on around him, sitting with a tense frown, staring out angrily at the world. Other times he deliberately turned away from Amy or his mother or lashed out angrily at the staff trying to help him. It was difficult for Amy to believe he'd ever regain his balance.

❧

Working with the horses was just the distraction Amy needed. When she was at Heartland, she felt certain that Ty would be back.

One evening, she was riding Blackjack down to the big training ring for some exercise. Blackjack continued to make great progress. He was relaxed and happy now, and he was no longer aggressive when in his stall. Amy reached the ring and found Ben schooling Red over a course of jumps.

"Is it OK if I work Blackjack at this end?" she called to him.

"Sure," Ben called back.

As a test of Blackjack's patience and cooperation, Amy unlatched the gate while she was mounted, asking the horse to be patient and then negotiate his way around the entry. He sidestepped neatly to allow her to pull the gate closed, and Amy smiled in satisfaction. Blackjack knew perfectly well what to do and how to behave — he was an old hand, really. He just didn't like being bullied or treated clumsily, year after year, by novice riders who didn't know any better.

"It's a shame we can't keep you," murmured Amy, patting him on the neck as she shut the gate and pushed him into a trot around the ring. Out of the corner of her eye, Amy was aware of Ben and Red flying over the jumps. After warming up with a few rounds of the ring, Amy pulled Blackjack up to watch for a moment. The jumps weren't as high as the ones that Ben would expect to see in a competition, and the course he had mapped out wasn't very long. Red could manage this easily, but Amy knew that wasn't the point. After a bout of the equine flu, it was important not to strain a horse's heart and lungs. Ben was getting it just right, not pushing too hard.

Nevertheless, Amy thought he looked frustrated. She waited until he'd completed the round, then called to him. "Red's doing well!" she shouted.

Ben nodded and trotted over. "Yeah, he's getting there."

"When do you think you'll be ready to show again?" Amy asked.

"For better or worse, I've signed up for a local show that's in two weeks," said Ben. "Just a Restricted Open Jumping class, to get us back into the swing of things."

"That's great news," Amy enthused. "Is it on a Saturday? I'd love to come and cheer you on. Storm might be there, too."

Ben smiled, then shrugged. "That's nice of you, Amy,"

he said in a slightly strained voice. "But I wouldn't expect you to. You've got too much going on."

"Sure, I'm busy," said Amy. "But this is a big thing for you, and it makes me happy to know things are getting back to where they should be. You and Red belong on the circuit."

Ben looked down and fiddled with his reins. "Sometimes I wonder if it's really worth it. What's the point?"

"Ben!" exclaimed Amy. "What are you getting at? I thought competing on Red was the most important thing in the world to you!"

Ben leaned down and stroked the chestnut horse's neck. Red snorted and played with the bit in his mouth. He was beautiful — so refined, well schooled, and strong. Amy knew he was devoted to his owner.

Ben shook his head a little helplessly. "It's just that sometimes I remember why I got into this in the first place. I mean, I started riding because I felt my mom didn't really care about me. I needed something that was mine."

Amy frowned. "What made you think of that?" she asked gently.

Ben shook his head. "I'm not sure I want to bother you with this, Amy," he said. "You've got enough problems to deal with."

Amy looked at Ben sitting on his horse and was suddenly struck by how alone he seemed. Ever since the storm and Ty's accident, he'd been so strong — supportive, helpful, and incredibly hardworking. But it occurred to Amy that there was no one around to support *him*.

"Please don't worry about that, Ben," she said. "You've been so great to me. I want to help if I can. We all have problems, not just me. You know you can talk to me anytime."

"I guess," said Ben. He hesitated, then sighed. "It has to do with Soraya," he admitted.

"Soraya?" Amy questioned. She stared at Ben. It was all starting to make sense. Soraya had liked him ever since he'd started working at Heartland, and she'd done her best to show it in little ways. She'd gone with him to shows, been on trail rides, worked with him around the yard, and they'd always gotten along well. They'd even flirted with each other on and off.

"I'm too late, aren't I?" said Ben bleakly. "I get the feeling she's not interested anymore."

Amy wasn't sure what to say. Ben was right. Soraya *had* lost interest, and what's more, she was now pursuing someone else.

"I always thought I had plenty of time," Ben carried on. "I wanted to focus on Red. I didn't want any distractions. I thought it'd be better to take things slowly. But when Red got sick, I realized how narrow-minded I had been. He is all I have. So I thought maybe I'd see how things were with Soraya, but even then, I wasn't in a hurry."

"Oh, Ben," said Amy sympathetically. "I'm sorry . . . I wish . . . "

"So I'm right then," said Ben, interrupting her. "There's no chance."

Feeling desperately sorry for him, Amy shook her head. "I think you should let it go," she admitted. "So-raya's really tied up with stuff at school. People move on from things, you know? It's just not a good time."

Ben nodded, looking Amy directly in the eyes. "I'm guessing there's someone else," he said.

Amy hesitated, not certain how to respond. "Yes," she said honestly. "It hasn't really started yet, but . . . "

"Right. I kind of figured," said Ben. He stroked Red's mane absentmindedly.

Amy wished she could offer more comfort, but there was no point in pretending. Soraya and Matt were getting closer all the time. They even made Amy feel left out sometimes.

Amy was glad Ben had been willing to tell her what was bothering him, but finding out about his feelings for Soraya almost made her feel worse. She had thought she was the only one feeling isolated and alone, but Ben had been lonely, too. And she hadn't even realized it.

"Thanks for telling me, Ben," said Amy. "Sorry I don't have better news." She paused, thinking. "You know, I think what you said is true. You missed a chance, but it was because you were concentrating on something else.

And that's not necessarily a bad thing. I guess you need to decide what's most important to you."

Ben looked thoughtful. "I see what you're saying," he said. "If Red comes first, everything else is going to come second. It makes sense."

"But maybe not always," suggested Amy. "He's first now, but you might prioritize differently at some point."

Ben nodded. "That's a good way of looking at it," he mused.

Amy tried her best to give Ben a reassuring smile, then gathered Blackjack's reins. He had almost gone to sleep, but Red was pawing the ground and beginning to prance on the spot. Ben patted the chestnut's neck and nudged him forward. "I'd better get him moving again. Can't have him think I'm neglecting him."

He turned Red around and headed back toward the jumps.

It was almost dark by the time Amy had finished with Blackjack, but after putting him away she walked down to Dazzle's paddock. Now that the stallion was showing signs of responding to her, she wanted to visit him as often as possible, both in the mornings and the evenings, even if it was only for ten minutes or so.

"Hey, Dazzle," she called from the gate.

The mustang raised his head and nickered a greeting.

Amy let herself into the paddock and walked toward him slowly and steadily. Dazzle allowed her to approach, but she knew she couldn't push it too far. A few yards in front of him, she stopped.

"Hello, boy," she said, standing still so that she posed no threat. "Will you let me come closer?"

Dazzle snorted at the sound of her voice and shook himself. In the half-light, his eyes looked big and luminous, but there was no sign of fear. Amy took one step closer, then decided she had reached the limit of what he would accept. Any farther and he might pull away and retreat from her, a risk she didn't want to take. She stood for a minute longer, then turned her back, sagging her shoulders slightly so that, once again, he knew she was not an aggressor.

This was similar to the second stage of join up — the moment of turning away and giving the horse a choice either to remain alone or to follow the person and become friends. It was a choice Amy presented every time she came to the paddock, and she sensed that the mustang was gradually getting closer to following her. But tonight he stayed where he was, watching her as she walked slowly back to the gate.

She headed to the barns and did a final round of all the stalls before going inside for dinner. Things were going well for most of the other horses. She decided it was time to tell Lou that Blackjack could go back to his owners.

Solly continued to do well and didn't seem to be missing Willow too much. Silver was growing in confidence daily. Nearly all the horses were heading in the right direction.

The one horse that still remained problematic was Candy. The mare had certainly quieted down since her case of the flu, but there were still moments when she resisted her rider for all she was worth — particularly when she was around other horses. Amy recalled how she had acted up when Dazzle first arrived, and the mare had recently snapped at Red, too. It could be a real problem for her owner at shows, where a single misstep could ruin Candy's chances in a dressage class.

❧

A few nights later, Amy was feeling optimistic as she made her way to the hospital. Ty was getting easier to be with. His moods were becoming more predictable, and he could manage basic tasks now, such as holding a fork and brushing his teeth. His legs were getting stronger, and the physical therapist, Clare, had assured Amy that he should be able to walk again before long. It seemed to Amy that one thing was still particularly difficult for Ty. He hadn't said a lot, and when he did, his speech was stilted, with certain sounds being harder to pronouce than others.

Amy walked through the hospital's familiar doors and took the elevator up to the third floor. It was all so automatic now. She turned into Ty's room, humming a tune.

Ty was sitting up in bed, but he didn't seem to realize she was there. "Ty?" Amy said questioningly.

Ty turned toward her. His eyes lit up when he saw her, and a smile spread across his face. "Amy," he said slowly.

Amy smiled back and went to sit by the side of his bed. She reached for Ty's hand and grasped it. As he gripped hers in return and smiled again, Amy felt content. She sat and began to chat about the horses at Heartland. She told him about Dazzle's progress and how so many of the horses were doing well. She was glad to share good news.

"But there's still Candy," Amy continued. "I can't seem to get anywhere with her. She only sidesteps and acts up occasionally since having the flu, so it's difficult to get a handle on it. She's definitely not cured. Maybe it's like an anxiety disorder that kicks in when she's around other horses."

Amy studied Ty's face. She wasn't sure how much he could understand. He seemed to be listening, his brow creased in contemplation. Then he raised his head and looked at her. He seemed to be trying to tell her something. "Ho — bs," he said.

Amy didn't hear him clearly. She shook her head and leaned forward. "Sorry, Ty. I don't understand. What are you trying to say?"

Ty's face was furrowed with effort and frustration. "Ho — hops," he said.

"Hops?" repeated Amy, her heart giving a little leap as she put it together. "Did you say *hops*?"

Ty gave a broad smile and nodded.

Hops. Of course! Dried hops were ideal for Candy. They helped a horse recover from illness, and they could work wonders for horses with anxiety issues. Candy's problems didn't seem to have any deeper underlying cause. Amy knew it was possible for high-strung horses to display anxious, fractious behavior, and hops would be an effective remedy.

Amy was delighted that they might have found a solution for Candy, but the remedy wasn't what gave her complete joy. To her, the most important thing was that Ty remembered. She couldn't believe it. He *remembered* — the horses, the treatments, the life he'd had before. She leaned forward, wrapped her arms around his shoulders and hugged him. Then she sat up again and looked into his eyes.

"Ty," she said softly, "I love you. Do you remember?"

Ty's eyes held her gaze steadily. He nodded slowly. "Love . . . you," he replied.

Chapter Eleven

"Amy! Phone!" Grandpa's voice called from the farm-house doorway. "It's Ty's mom."

It was three weeks later. Ty had been making rapid progress, and the hospital was finally letting him go home to be cared for by his mom. Amy was hoping that Ty's doctors would permit him to stop at Heartland on the way — he had said he wanted to see all the horses, especially Dazzle.

Amy quickly tied Solly to a ring outside the stable block and ran inside.

"Hi, Mrs. Baldwin," she said. "How are the plans coming? Are you going to be able to stop by?"

"Yes, it's all worked out," said Ty's mom happily. "I've changed my shift at work. We'll plan to be there tomorrow about two o'clock. Will that be OK? We probably won't stay much more than an hour."

"That's perfect!" exclaimed Amy. "Thanks so much, Mrs. Baldwin. I'll start telling everyone."

Amy put down the phone and ran across the kitchen to hug Lou. "Ty's going to come here on his way home from the hospital!" she sang, twirling Lou around. "We should plan a welcome party!"

Lou laughed and nodded. "Of course," she agreed. "I'll start making calls. Who should I tell?"

Amy thought for a minute, her eyes shining. She couldn't believe this moment had finally arrived. "Well, Scott and Matt, of course," she said. "I'll tell Soraya myself. Nick Halliwell and Daniel. Ben will already be here. What about Nancy?"

"I'm sure she'd love to be included," smiled Lou. "I'll talk to Grandpa."

"Fantastic. I'll go and tell Ben." Amy rushed back out, her heart singing.

✇

That evening, Amy, Lou, and Soraya made a long banner out of an old sheet and wrote on it, in big red letters, WELCOME BACK, TY. Then, the following morning, Ben helped Lou and Amy tie it across the overhang of the front stable block. Amy ran around pinning streamers between the stalls. Lou found a packet of balloons and took them outside.

"How about these?" she suggested.

"Probably not," Amy said, shaking her head. "Gold Dust's a lot less jumpy, but we shouldn't risk it!"

"Point taken," Lou acknowledged. "You know, it's almost twelve already. I'll start making some lunch."

As Lou headed indoors, Amy looked at the decorations with satisfaction. Heartland looked so bright and festive — a place of happiness, where horses *and people* really could get better. She smiled, then headed toward the tack room. There was just enough time to lunge Candy before lunch.

Since Ty had made his suggestion, Amy had added dried hops to the mare's feed every day, and over the past few weeks, her moods had settled enormously. She was much calmer, and her fidgeting and temperamental outbursts seemed to be under control. Amy's heart swelled with pride at the thought that Ty had helped cure her. Heartland was almost back to the way it had been.

❧

Everyone arrived well before two o'clock to welcome Ty. Mrs. Baldwin's car pulled in right on time, and as she drove slowly to the house, the crowd erupted in a great big cheer and round of applause. They all gathered eagerly around the car as Mrs. Baldwin helped Ty into his wheelchair.

Even as he struggled to get his legs in place, Ty looked happy, his face fixed in a permanent grin. "It's . . . good to be back," he said, once he was settled into the chair. He looked around at the sea of faces. "Thought . . . I might not see Heart — Heartland again."

"None of *us* doubted it for a minute," said Lou firmly.

Amy looked at her sister, thinking how supportive she had been. Now that Ty was finally back, Amy was able to feel relief. Studying each face in the gathering, she realized everyone there had given her strength and hope. It was wonderful to share this moment with them.

"Come on, I'll introduce you to the new arrivals," said Amy eagerly, pushing the wheelchair forward. "And I think there will be some old friends who will be happy to see you."

Everyone followed, chatting happily, as Amy pushed Ty around the front yard. She introduced him to all the horses, then headed toward the back barn. The group grew silent as Ty stared at the building, now repaired. There were new support beams, and the entire roof had been replaced, along with the big timber doors. In its restored state, it was hard to believe how much damage there had been.

Ty shook his head. "I'm lucky," he said simply.

"We're the lucky ones," Ty's mom responded. "Lucky to have you back."

As they headed toward the paddocks, the others fell back, sensing they should allow Amy and Ty to have some time alone. "I'll take you to see Dazzle," Amy told Ty. "He almost likes people now."

Ty nodded.

To Amy's delight, Dazzle had heard the noise of their approach and was standing near the gate, looking curious. His ears were pricked forward and he sniffed the air, then nickered a welcome.

Amy pushed the wheelchair slowly. She wasn't sure how the stallion would react. He had grown to accept her presence and even allowed her to stroke his neck, but his wild nervousness was still never far from the surface. He might react to anything — the rattle of the wheelchair or an unfamiliar voice. Amy murmured to him reassuringly as they drew closer.

Dazzle snorted and took a few steps backward as Amy maneuvered the chair so that Ty could reach through the gate. Then, once they were still, Dazzle stretched out his neck in curiosity.

"Come on, boy," said Amy encouragingly. "This is Ty. Come and say hello."

Tentatively, Dazzle stepped forward again, his nostrils flaring with each breath. Ty looked the stallion over, then looked up at Amy.

"He's amazing," he said.

Ty held out his hand. Dazzle cautiously considered it and then gently blew over his palm. A smile spread across Ty's face as the stallion started to playfully lip his fingers. Amy's heart warmed at the sight. However long it was going to take Ty to get back on his feet — to be back to himself — one thing was the same: He hadn't lost his touch with horses.

The next week flew by as Ty gradually adjusted to being out of the hospital. At first, Mrs. Baldwin would bring him to Heartland for short stretches of time, but after a week Ty had developed more endurance and could stay for hours. One day, about two weeks after Ty's release, Amy watched from Solly's stall as Ben helped Ty apply saddle soap to Silver's saddle. Amy had been picking Solly's hooves, but she heard the two boys talking and looked around the corner curiously.

Ty's expression was full of concentration and determination as he began the job of rubbing the soap into the leather, a sponge grasped tightly between his fingers. Ben watched and candidly chatted with Ty about Red's progress. At the same time, he kept one hand on the back of the saddle, making sure it remained balanced on the arms of Ty's wheelchair. He passed his friend more saddle soap as needed.

"Red just loves being back on the circuit," Ben was saying. "It's like going home for him. He's almost fit again. The problem is, he's so excited when he gets to a show that he gets careless. I think it's going to take a few more shows for him to calm down and find his rhythm again."

"You could try giving him some chamomile powder just before a show," suggested Ty slowly. "That should help him relax."

"That's a good idea," said Ben thoughtfully. "I'll try that."

Ty looked at Ben, but as he did so, he lost grip of the sponge. He lunged forward to catch it but ended up knocking the saddle off the arm of his chair. "No!" he growled, frustration overwhelming him.

"It's OK," said Ben calmly. He repositioned the saddle and picked up the sponge. "Here you go. No harm done."

Ty accepted the sponge back, shaking his head. "I *hate* that," he said, his voice disconsolate.

"Come on, don't worry. You're getting there," said Ben. He grinned at Ty. "Don't rush it. You're like Red. So happy to be back, you forget that everything takes time."

At that, Ty relaxed again and nodded toward Ben. Amy smiled and quietly withdrew back into Solly's stall. Ben was right. Ty *was* getting there. Best of all, he was getting on well with the horses, particularly Dazzle. He wasn't able do much physical work yet, but he could be around the horses, and that was ideal for creating a bond with Dazzle. The mustang seemed to respond to Ty instinctively.

Amy let herself out of Solly's stall and walked over to Ty. "I've got to head off soon," she said. "I'm going to see the matinee of *Romeo and Juliet* at school. Will you guys be OK here while I'm gone?"

Ben's face tightened slightly at the mention of the play, but he smiled easily. Ever since Ty had returned to Heartland, Ben had seemed much happier. It was as though Ty's presence had put everything back into perspective. "Sure, we can cope, Amy," he said. "Go and have some fun."

Ty's eyes met Amy's and he laughed. "Sure, we'll take care of all the work," he joked.

Amy leaned down and kissed him on the cheek. "I hope so," she said. "I expect it to be all done by the time I get back. See you guys later."

She went inside to change and then, feeling lighthearted, caught the bus into town. She was really looking forward to the performance. It made a great change from her work at Heartland, but more important, it felt incredible knowing that there was nothing to worry about while she was gone. She had so much more time now that Ty was out of hospital, and everyone's spirits had lifted with him visiting every day.

Amy slipped into the back of the auditorium and found herself a good seat. She was glad she'd arrived in plenty of time; the hall was filling up fast. She hoped that Soraya and Matt weren't suffering from precurtain jitters backstage. They had both put in so much time rehearsing that Amy was certain they would perform well.

She was right. Soraya made a stunning Juliet with her dark eyes and curls. But Amy thought it was more than that — Soraya was simply radiant. She was captivating onstage, and it seemed like it was more than a good performance. Amy felt she was seeing her friend in a whole new way. And the chemistry between Soraya and Matt, as Romeo, was impossible to deny. Amy felt privileged to be their friend; they were both so talented. *And so good for each other,* she thought.

The curtains came down to thunderous applause. The ovation continued as the curtain rose for a second time. Soraya and Matt came back onstage and joined the rest of the cast for a final bow. Amy felt a rush of pride when Soraya looked her way and gave a discreet wave. As soon as the applause died down, Amy followed the audience out and went to congratulate her friends backstage.

She found the cast chatting excitedly, each member

surrounded by a cluster of admirers. Amy spotted So-raya, holding a bouquet of flowers from a fan, close to the stage door. Amy drew closer but lingered on the outside of the group, not sure whether to interrupt. As soon as Soraya spotted her, she politely excused herself.

"Amy!" she exclaimed and rushed over. "I'm so glad you came. Thank you!"

"You were fantastic," praised Amy. "I'm so proud of you. You and Matt were amazing."

"Oh, Amy", said Soraya dreamily, her eyes shining. "I am just so happy — and relieved. I mean, it's great that the play went well and everything, but it's more than that."

"No, wait. Don't tell me. I think I can guess," said Amy, smiling and shaking her head as Matt came up and put his arm around Soraya. "It's about time."

"How'd you know?" Soraya asked.

Amy laughed. "I think everyone in the audience could probably put it together."

"Well, it's official," said Matt. He looked at his watch and raised an eyebrow toward Soraya. "I think it's been just about . . . five hours."

"No wonder you gave such an amazing performance!" Amy said, hugging Soraya.

"What? Are you doubting our natural theatrical talent?" asked Matt in mock dismay. "Soraya, are you going to stand for that?"

"I don't mind," responded Soraya cheerily. "I think it'll be a happy ending as long as I get something to eat — soon. Amy, we were thinking of going for pizza. Want to join us?"

"No, that's OK," Amy replied. "You go ahead."

It was almost dark when Amy got home. On the bus, she thought about how happy Soraya and Matt seemed. She remembered what it had been like when she and Ty had first started seeing each other, as their friendship grew into something more. And she remembered the promises she had made when he was in the hospital. They had been through a lot, and she had been so concerned about so many things along the way. She hoped that Ty's mom hadn't already come by to pick him up — she so wanted to see him before he left, to tell him again how happy she was that he was back. She stood up, eager for her stop. After climbing down the bus steps, she started to jog up the driveway. She found Ben in the grain room preparing the evening feeds.

"Hey," she said. "Is Ty still here?"

"Yeah. He's down with Dazzle," answered Ben. "Did you have a good time?"

"Great," said Amy. She hesitated for a moment, then added, "I think Soraya's headed for Hollywood."

"Good for her," said Ben warmly. "Give her my congratulations next time you see her."

"I will," promised Amy. "And you and Red are still on for the Millbrook Classic next week?"

"That's the plan."

"Well, Ty and I will be there, too, cheering you on," Amy said.

"We'll take all the help we can get," Ben replied with a smile.

Amy left the feed room and headed down to the pastures in the fading light. The November evening was crisp, and her breath formed a white haze in the cold air. Then, as she neared the paddock, her heart suddenly stopped. She could just see the outline of Ty's wheelchair — empty. She gasped and ran forward. Had something happened?

Relief flooded over her as she focused on Ty's figure. He was standing up, by himself, leaning against the gate to the paddock. Dazzle was there, too, his muzzle reaching over the fence as Ty gently stroked his neck.

Ty turned at the sound of Amy's footsteps.

"You're back!" he called, smiling, as Dazzle nickered a greeting.

Amy rushed toward him. As she reached the gate, she gave Dazzle a pat and put her arms around Ty. She held him tight. When she finally let go, she leaned against the fence next to him and wrapped her fingers around his. They stood there with Dazzle in silence, and Amy tried to let it all sink in. The warmth of Ty's hand. The sound of Dazzle's easy breathing. The familiar scent of a crisp autumn evening.

Amy knew that there would always be changes. The past two years had certainly taught her that. But she also knew that there was nothing about this moment that she would ever want to change. And in her memories, she hoped it would always feel the same.

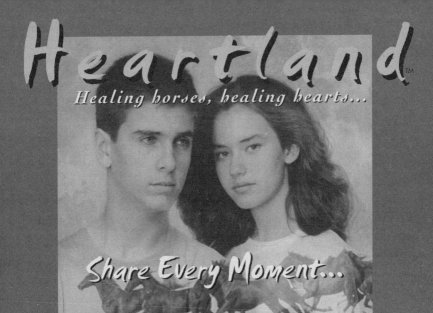

PRAIRIE RIVER

A JOURNEY OF FAITH

Kristiana Gregory

The year is 1865 and Nessa Clemens is about to turn 14. On her birthday she'll have no choice but to leave the orphanage she's called home for as long as she can remember. Her plan is to escape on the next stagecoach heading west to Prairie River—a town in the middle of nowhere. She doesn't have a job or a home, and she doesn't know anyone, but her faith tells her that everything is going to be all right.

www.scholastic.com/books

Available wherever books are sold.

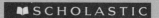